"No, Maksim. I Refuse Your New Deal."

"It's a proposal, Caliope."

She took a step back, then another, making him feel she was receding forever out of reach. "Whatever you want to call it, my answer is still no. And it's a final no. You had no right to think you can seek redemption at my expense."

"The redemption I'm seeking is for you. I'm offering you everything I can, what you just admitted you need."

"I only said you left at a time when I most needed you, not that I need you still."

Every word fell on him like a lash, their pain accumulating until he was numb. But after leaving her, how could he have hoped for anything different?

* * *

Claiming His Own is part of the #1 bestselling miniseries from Harlequin Desire—

Billionaires and Babies: Powerful men... wrapped around their babies' little fingers

* * *

D1462917

Dear Reader,

I have loved each and every book I've written, given each line everything that I had and have become truly attached to every couple whose passionate story I've told.

But every now and then there comes a book where everything comes together as if by magic, from the premise to the characters, the conflict to the black moment, to the hard-won resolution.

Claiming His Own was such a book. Every single word came to me with such certainty, such intensity, that once I'd put down the words, I didn't have to stop to second-guess or even to polish what I'd written. It truly felt as if I was just a bystander watching Maksim's and Caliope's heart-wrenching love story unfold, listening to their innermost turmoil and experiencing their heartfelt desires and fears, and capturing every detail just as it came into existence.

I so hope you enjoy their story as much as I did, live with them every second of their fervent love and passion, and be as deeply touched as I was by their ordeals and triumphs.

I love to hear from readers, so please contact me at oliviagates@gmail.com. Connect with me on Facebook, at www.facebook.com/oliviagatesauthor, and on Twitter, @OliviaGates.

To find out about my latest releases, to read excerpts and sign up for giveaways, please visit www.oliviagates.com.

Enjoy, and thanks for reading.

Olivia Gates

CLAIMING
HIS OWN

—

OLIVIA GATES

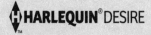

Recycling programs
for this product may
not exist in your area.

ISBN-13: 978-0-373-73278-4

CLAIMING HIS OWN

Copyright © 2013 by Olivia Gates

This edition published by arrangement with Harlequin Books S.A.

For questions and comments about the quality of this book, please contact us at CustomerService@Harlequin.com.

Printed in U.S.A.

www.Harlequin.com

OLIVIA GATES

has always pursued creative passions such as singing and handicrafts. She still does, but only one of her passions grew gratifying enough, consuming enough, to become an ongoing career—writing.

She is most fulfilled when she is creating worlds and conflicts for her characters, then exploring and untangling them bit by bit, sharing her protagonists' every heart-wrenching heartache and hope, their every heart-pounding doubt and trial, until she leads them to an indisputably earned and gloriously satisfying happy ending.

When she's not writing, she is a doctor, a wife to her own alpha male and a mother to one brilliant girl and one demanding Angora cat. Visit Olivia at www.oliviagates.com.

To my brother. Thanks for being you. Everyone who's ever known you will understand just what I mean.

Prologue

Eighteen months ago

Caliope Sarantos stared at the strip in her hand.

It was the third one so far. The two pink lines had appeared in each, glaring and undeniable.

She was pregnant.

Even though she'd been meticulous about birth control, she just…was.

A dozen conflicting emotions frothed over again, colliding inside her chest. Whatever she did about this, it would turn her world upside down, would probably shatter the perfection she'd forged with Maksim. If *she* didn't know what to feel about this, what would he…

Suddenly her heart fired so hard, she almost keeled over.

He was here.

As always, she felt Maksim before she heard him. Her whole being surged with worry this time rather than welcome. Once she told him, nothing would remain the same.

He walked into the bedroom where he'd first taught her what passion was, where he continued to show her there was no limit to the intimacies and pleasures they could share.

His wolf's eyes sizzled with passion as he strode toward her, throwing away his tie and attacking his shirt as if it burned him. He was starving for her, as usual. But what she'd tell him was bound to extinguish his urgency. An unplanned pregnancy was the last thing he expected.

This might end everything between them.

This could be her last time with him.

She couldn't tell him. Not before she had him.

Desperate desire erupted, consuming her sanity as she met his urgency with her own, pulling him down to the bed on top of her, trembling with the enormity of having him in her arms. His lips fused to hers, his rumble of voracity and enjoyment pouring into her, spiking her arousal. Before she wrapped herself around him, he yanked her up, bent her over one arm, had her breasts jutting in an erotic offering. Pouring litanies of craving all over her, he kneaded her breasts, pulling her nipples into the moist heat of his mouth, sucking with such perfect force that each pull had her screams of pleasure rising. Then he glided a hand over her abdomen until he squeezed her trim mound.

Just as she screamed again, he slid two fingers between the slickness of her folds, growling again as her arousal perfumed the air.

With only a few strokes, he had her senses overloading and release scorching through her body in waves, from his fondling fingers outwards. He completed her climax with rough encouragements before he slid down her body, coming between her shaking legs, spreading them over his shoulders, exploiting her every inch with hands, lips and teeth until she was thrashing again.

"Please, enough," she moaned. "I need you…."

He subdued her with a hand flat on her abdomen, his face set in imperious lines. "Let me have my fill of your pleasure. Open for me, Caliope."

His command had her legs falling apart, surrendering everything to him. He latched on to her core, drank her flowing essence and arousal until she felt her body would unravel with the need for release. As if he knew the exact moment when she couldn't take any more, he tongued her, and she cried herself hoarse on a chain reaction of convulsions.

Before her rioting breath had a chance to subside, he slid up her sweat-slick body, flattening her to the bed. Her breath hitched and her dropping heat shot up again as soon as his tongue filled her, feeding her his taste mingled with that of her pleasure. It was unbelievable how he ignited her with only a touch.

He fused their lips for feverish seconds before he reared up, his eyes searching hers, his erection seeking her entrance. Finding both her eyes and her core molten, he growled his surrender and sank into her.

She cried out at the first inevitable shock of his invasion, that craved expansion of her flesh as it yielded to his daunting potency and poured more readiness to welcome him.

He groaned his own agonized pleasure as he rose to his knees between her splayed thighs, cupped her hips and thrust himself to the hilt inside her, hitting that trigger inside her that always made her go wild beneath him.

Knowing just what to do to wreak havoc on her senses, he withdrew, plunged again and again until her breath became fevered snatches and she writhed against him, demanding that he end his exquisite torment. Only then did he give her his full ferocity, in ram after jarring ram, in the exact force and cadence she was dying for.

He escalated to a jackhammering tempo inside her until she shrieked, arched in a spastic bow, crushed herself to him as pleasure detonated her, undoing her to her very cells.

Through the delirium she heard him roar, felt his great body shuddering, his seed splashing against her intimate flesh, dousing the inferno that threatened to turn her to ashes. She held on to awareness, to him, until he collapsed on top of her, filling her trembling arms, before she spiraled into an abyss of satiation, hitting bottom bonelessly, consciousness dissipating....

She came back into her body with a gasp as, still fused to her, he rose above her, his breathing as labored as hers, his eyes crackling with satisfaction, melting with indulgence, his lips flushed and swollen with the savagery of their coupling. He looked heartbreakingly virile and vital, and he was...hers.

She'd never allowed herself to think of him this way... but he was.

Since she'd met him, Maksim Volkov had been hers alone.

Though she'd long known of him, the Russian steel tycoon who was on par with her eldest brother, Aristedes, as one of the world's richest and most powerful men, it had taken that first face-to-face glance across the room at that charity gala a year ago for a certainty to come to her fully formed. That he'd turn her life upside down. If she let him.

And she'd let him, and then some.

She still remembered with acute intensity how she'd breathlessly allowed him to kiss her within minutes of meeting, how he'd claimed her lips, thrust his tongue inside her gasping mouth, fed her the ambrosia of his taste, turned her into a mass of mindlessness. She'd never imagined she could feel anything so suffocating in intensity, so transporting in headiness. She'd never imagined she could need a man to take her over, to dominate her.

And within an hour, she'd let him sweep her to his presidential hotel suite, knowing that she'd allow him every intimacy there. It had only been on the way there in his ultimate luxury Mercedes that she'd regained enough presence of mind to tell him that she was a virgin, even when she'd been dreading that the revelation would end their magical encounter prematurely.

She'd never forgotten his reaction.

The banked fire in his eyes had flared again as he took her lips again in a kiss that was possession itself, a sealing of her surrender.

As he'd released her and before he'd set the car in motion, he'd pledged, "It's my unparalleled privilege to be your first, Caliope. And I'm going to make it your unimaginable pleasure."

And how he'd fulfilled his pledge. It had been so overwhelming between them, they'd both known that a one-night stand was out of the question. But because of the disastrous example of her own parents, then the disappointing track records of almost everyone she knew, she believed commitment was just a setup for anything from mind-numbing mediocrity to soul-destroying disappointment. She'd never felt the least temptation to risk either.

But wanting more of Maksim had gone beyond temptation into compulsion. The very intensity of her need had made it imperative she make sure their liaison didn't take a turn in the wrong direction.

To ensure that, she'd demanded rules, upfront and unswerving, to govern whatever time they had together. They'd be together whenever their schedules allowed. For as long as they shared the same level of passion and pleasure, felt the same eagerness for each other. But once the fire was gone, they'd say goodbye amicably and move on.

He had agreed to her terms but had added his own non-negotiable one. Exclusivity.

Stunned that he'd propose or want that, with his reputation as a notorious playboy, it had only made her plunge harder, deeper, until she'd lost herself in what raged between them. But all the time she'd wondered how long it could possibly last. Not even in her wildest dreams had she hoped it would burn that brightly for long, let alone indefinitely.

But it was now a year later and it kept growing more powerful between them, blazing ever hotter.

And she couldn't lose him. She *couldn't*.

But she had to tell him…

"I'm pregnant."

Her heart hammered painfully as even she was taken aback at her own raggedly blurted out declaration. Then more as silence exploded in its wake.

It was as if he'd turned to stone. Nothing remained animate in him except his eyes. And the expression that crashed into them was enough.

Any unformed hope she might have held—that the pregnancy might lead to something more for them—died an abrupt and agonizing death.

Suddenly, she felt she'd suffocate under his weight. Sensing her distress, he lurched off her. She groaned with the pain of separation as he left her body for what was probably the last time.

She sat up unsteadily, groping for the covers. "You don't need to concern yourself with this. Being pregnant is my business, as it is my business that I decided to have the baby. I only thought it was your right to know. Just as it is your right to feel and act as you wish concerning the fact."

His grimness was absolute as he, too, sat up, as if rising from under rubble. "You don't want me near your baby."

Did her words make him think that she didn't?

She forced out a whispered qualification through her

closing throat. "It is your baby, too. I welcome your role in its life, whatever you want it to be."

"I mean you *don't* want me near your baby. Or you as a new mother. I'm not a man to be trusted in such situations. I *will* give the baby my name, make it my heir. But I will never take part in its upbringing." Before she could gasp out her confusion over his contradicting statements, he carried on, "But I want to remain your lover. For as long as you'll have me. When you no longer want me, I'll stay away. You will both have my limitless support always, but I cannot be involved in your daily lives."

He reached for her, his eyes piercing her with their vehemence. "This is all I can offer. This is what I am, Caliope. And I can't change."

She stared up into his fierce gaze, knowing one thing. That the sane thing to do was to refuse his offer. The self-preserving thing was to cut him off from her life now, not later.

But she couldn't even contemplate doing that. Whatever damage it caused in the future, she couldn't sacrifice what she could have of him in the present to avoid it.

And she succumbed to his new terms.

But as the weeks passed, she kept bating her breath wondering if she'd been wrong to succumb. And right in believing the pregnancy would shatter their perfection.

She did sense his withdrawal in everything he said and did. But he confused her even more when he always came back hungrier than ever.

Then just as she entered her seventh month, and was more confused than ever about where they stood, her world stopped turning completely when Maksim just… disappeared.

One

"And he never came back?"

Cali stared at Kassandra Stavros's gorgeous face. It took several disconcerted moments before she reminded herself her new friend couldn't possibly be talking about Maksim.

After all, Kassandra didn't even know about him. No one did.

Cali had kept their…liaison a secret from her family and friends. Even when declaring her pregnancy had become unavoidable, with Maksim still in her life, she'd refused to tell anyone who the father was. Even when she'd clung to the hope that he'd remain part of her life after her baby was born, their situation had been too…irregular, and she'd had no wish to explain it to anyone. Certainly not to her traditional Greek family.

The only one she knew who wouldn't have judged was Aristedes. Her, that was. He would have probably wanted to take Maksim apart. Literally. When he'd been in a similar situation, her brother had gone to extreme lengths to stake a claim on his lover, Selene, and their son, Alex. He'd consider any man doing anything less a criminal. His outrage would have been a thousand fold with her and his nephew on the other end of the equation. Aristedes would have probably exacted a drastic punishment on Maksim for shirking his responsibilities. Knowing Maksim, it would have developed into a war.

Not that she would have tolerated being considered Maksim's "responsibility," or would have let Aristedes fight her battle. Not when it hadn't been one to start with. She'd told Maksim he'd owed her nothing. And she'd meant it. As for Aristedes and her family, she'd been independent far too long to want their blessings or need their support. She wouldn't have let anyone have an opinion, let alone a say, in how she'd conducted her life, or the… arrangement she'd had with Maksim.

Then he'd disappeared, making the whole thing redundant. All they knew was that Leo's father had been "nothing serious."

Kassandra was now talking about another man in Cali's life who'd been a living example of "nothing serious." Someone who should also hold some record for Most Callous User.

Her father.

The only good thing he'd ever done, in her opinion, had been leaving her mother and his brood of kids before Cali had been born. Her other siblings, especially Aristedes and Andreas, had lifelong scars to account for their exposure to his negligence and exploitation. She'd at least escaped that.

She finally answered her friend, sighing, "No. He was gone one day and was never heard from again. We have no idea if he's still alive. Though he must be long dead or he would have surfaced as soon as Aristedes made his first ten thousand dollars."

Her friend's mouth dropped open. "You think he would have come back asking for money? From the son he'd abandoned?"

"Can't imagine that type of malignant nonparent, huh?"

Kassandra shrugged. "Guess I can't. My father and uncles may be controlling Greek pains, but it's because they're really hopeless mother hens."

Cali smiled, seeing how any male in the family of the incredibly beautiful Kassandra would be protective of her. "According to Selene, they believe you give them just cause for their Greek overprotectiveness to go into hyperdrive."

A chuckle burst on Kassandra's lips. "Selene told you about them, huh?"

Selene, Aristedes's wife and Kassandra's best friend, had told her the broad lines about Kassandra before introducing them to each other, confident they'd work spectacularly well together. Which they did. But they'd only started being more than business associates in the past two months, gradually becoming close personal friends. Which Cali welcomed very much. She did need a woman to talk to, one of her own age, temperament and interests, and Kassandra fulfilled all those criteria. Although Selene certainly fit the bill, too, ever since Cali had given birth to Leo, being around family, which Selene was now, had become too…uncomfortable.

So Kassandra had been heaven-sent. And though they'd been delving deeper in private waters every time they met, it was the first time they'd swerved into the familial zone.

Glad to steer the conversation away from herself, she grinned at her new confidante. "Selene only told me the basics, said she'd leave it up to you to supply the hilarious details."

Kassandra slid lower on the couch, her incredible hair fanning out against the cushions in a glossy sun-streaked mass, her Mediterranean-green eyes twinkling in amusement. "Yeah, I flaunted their strict values, their conservative expectations and traditional hopes for me. I wasted one huge opportunity after another of acquiring a socially enviable, deep-pocketed 'sponsor' to procreate with, to provide them with more perfect, preferably male progenies to shove onto the path of greatness, following my brothers' and cousins' shiningly ruthless example, and to perpetuate the romantic, if misleading, stereotype of those almighty Greek tycoons."

Cali chuckled, Kassandra's dry wit tickling her almost atrophied sense of humor. "They must have had collective strokes when you left home at eighteen and worked your way through college in minimum-wage jobs and then added mortification to worry by becoming a model."

Kassandra grinned. "They do attribute their blood-pressure and sugar-level abnormalities to my scandalous behavior. You'd think they would have settled down now that I've hit thirty and left my lingerie-modeling days behind to become a struggling designer."

Kassandra was joking here since at thirty she was far more beautiful than she'd been at twenty. She'd just become so famous she preferred to model only for causes now. And she was well on her way to becoming just as famous as a designer. Cali felt privileged to be a major part of establishing her as a household name through an innovative series of online ad campaigns.

Kassandra's generous lips twisted. "But no. They're still recycling the same nightmares about the dangers I must be facing, fending off the perverts and predators they imagine populate my chosen profession. And they're lamenting my single status louder by the day, and getting more frantic as they count down my fast-fading attractions and fertility. Thirty to Greeks seems to be the equivalent of fifty in other cultures."

Cali snorted. "Next time they wail, point them my way.

They'd thank you instead for not detonating their social standing completely by bearing an out-of-wedlock child."

A wicked gleam deepened the emerald of Kassandra's eyes. "Maybe I should. It doesn't seem I'll ever find a man who'll mess with my mind enough that I'd actually be willing to put up with the calamity of the marriage institution either for real, or for the cause of perpetuating the Stavros species. Not to mention that your and Selene's phenomenal tykes are making my biological clock clang."

Cali's heart twitched. Whenever Kassandra lumped her with Selene, it brought their clashing realities into painful focus. Selene, having two babies with the love of her life. And her, having Leo…alone.

"Being a single parent isn't something to be considered lightly," she murmured.

Contrition filled Kassandra's eyes. "Which you are in the best position to know. I remember how Selene struggled before Aristedes came back. As successful as she is, being a single mother was such a big burden to bear alone. Before her experience, I had this conviction that fathers were peripheral at best in the first few years of a child's life. But then I saw the night-and-day difference Aristedes made in Selene and Alex's lives…." She huffed a laugh. "Though he's no example. We all know there's only one of him on planet earth."

Just as Cali had thought there was only one of Maksim. If not because of any human traits…

But Aristedes had once appeared to be just as inhuman. In his case, appearances had been the opposite of reality.

Cali sighed again. "You don't know how flabbergasted I still am sometimes to see how amazing Aristedes is as a husband and father. We used to believe he was the phenomenally successful version of our heartless, loser father."

It had been one specific night in particular that she'd become convinced of that. The night Leonidas—their brother—had died.

As she and her sisters had clung together, reeling from the horrific loss, Aristedes had swooped in and taken complete charge of the situation. All business, he'd dealt with the police and the burial and arranged the wake, but had offered them no solace, hadn't stayed an hour after the funeral.

That had still been far better than Andreas, who hadn't returned at all, or even acknowledged Leonidas's death then or since. But it had convinced her that Aristedes, too, had no emotions…just like their father.

She'd since realized that he was the opposite of their father, felt *too* much, but had been so unversed in demonstrating his emotions, he'd expressed them instead in the support he'd lavished on her and all his siblings since they'd been born. But after Selene had *claimed him,* as he said, something fundamental had changed in him. He was still ruthless in business, but on a personal level, he'd opened up with his family and friends. And when it came to Selene and their kids, he was a huge rattle toy.

"So your father was that bad, huh?" Kassandra asked.

Cali took a sip of tea, loath to discuss her father. She'd always been glib about him. But it was suddenly hitting her how close to her own situation it all was.

She exhaled her rising unease. "His total lack of morals and concern for anything beyond his own petty interests were legend. He got my mother pregnant with Aristedes when she was only seventeen. He was four years older, a charmer who never held down a job and who only married her because his father threatened to cut him off financially if he didn't. He used her and the kids he kept impregnating her with to squeeze his father for bigger allowances, which he spent on himself. After his father died, he took his inheritance and left."

Cali paused for a moment to regulate her agitated breathing before resuming. "He came back when he'd squandered it, knowing full well that Mother would feed him and take care of him with what little money she earned or got from those who remained of her own family, those who'd stopped helping out when they realized their hard-earned money was going to that user. He drifted in and out of her and my siblings' lives, each time coming back to add another child to his brood and another burden on my mother's shoulders before disappearing again. He always came back swearing his love, of course, offering sob stories about how hard life was on him."

Chagrin filled Kassandra's eyes more with every word. "And your mother just took him back?"

Cali nodded, more uncomfortable by the second at the associations this conversation was raising.

"Aristedes said she didn't know it was possible for her not to. He understood it all, having been forced to mature very early, but could do nothing about it except help his mother. He was only seven when he was already doing everything that no-good father should have been doing while mother took care of the younger kids. By twelve he had left school and was working four jobs to barely make ends meet. Then when he was fifteen, said non-father disappeared for the final time when I was still a work in progress.

"Aristedes went on to work his way up from the docks in Crete to become one of the biggest shipping magnates in the world. Regretfully, our mother was around only to see the beginnings of his success, as she died when I was only six. He then brought us all over here to New York, got us American citizenships and provided us with the best care and education money could buy.

"But he didn't stick around, didn't even become American himself, except after he married Selene. But his success and all that we have now was in spite of what that man who fathered us did to destroy our lives, as he managed to destroy our mother. All in all, I am only thankful I didn't have the curse of having him poison my life as he did Aristedes's and the rest of my siblings'."

Kassandra blinked, as if unable to take in that level of unfeeling, premeditated exploitation. "It's mind-boggling. How someone can be so…evil with those he's supposed to care for. He did one thing right, though, even if inadvertently. He had you and your siblings. You guys are great."

Cali refrained from telling her that she'd always thought only Leonidas had been deserving of that accolade. Now she knew Aristedes was, too, but she felt her three sisters, though she loved them dearly, had been infected with a degree or another of their mother's passivity and willingness to be downtrodden. Andreas, sibling number five out of seven, was just…an enigma. From his lifelong loath interactions with them, she was inclined to think that he was far worse than anything she'd ever thought Aristedes to be.

But while she'd thought she'd escaped her mother's infection, perhaps she hadn't after all.

Apart from the different details, Cali had basically done with Maksim what her mother had done with her father. She'd gotten involved with someone she'd known she shouldn't have. Then, when it had been in her best interest to walk away, she'd been too weak to do so, until he'd been the one who'd left her.

But her mother had had an excuse. An underprivileged woman living in Crete isolated from opportunity or hope of anything different, a woman who didn't know how to aspire to better.

Cali was a twenty-first-century, highly educated, totally independent American woman. How could she defend her actions and decisions?

"Look at the time!" Kassandra jumped to her feet. "Next time, just kick me out and don't let little ol' kidless me keep you from stocking up on sleep for those early mornings with Leo."

Rising, Cali protested, "I'd rather have you here all night yammering about anything than sleep. I've been starving for adult company…particularly of the female variety, outside of discussing baby stuff with Leo's nanny."

Kassandra hugged her, chuckling as she rushed to the door. "You can use me any time to ward off your starvation."

After setting up a meeting to discuss the next phase in their campaign and to go over Cali's progress reports, Kassandra rushed off, and Cali found herself staring at the closed oak door of her suddenly silent apartment.

That all-too-familiar feeling of dejection, which always assailed her when she didn't have a distraction, settled over her like a shroud.

She could no longer placate herself that this was lingering postpartum depression. She hated to admit it, but everything she'd been suffering for the past year had only one cause.

Maksim.

She walked back through her place, seeing none of its exquisiteness or the upgrades she'd installed to make it suitable for a baby. Her feet, as usual, took her without conscious volition to Leo's room.

She tiptoed inside, though she knew she wouldn't wake him. After the first six sleepless months, he'd thankfully switched to all-night-sleeping mode. She believed taking away the night-light and having him sleep in darkness had helped. She now only had the corridor light to guide her, though she'd know her way to his bed blindfolded.

As her vision adjusted, his beloved shape materialized out of the darkness, and emotion twisted in her throat as it always did whenever she beheld him. It regularly blindsided her, the power of her feelings for him.

He was so achingly beautiful, so frightfully perfect, she lived in dread of anything happening to him. She wondered if all mothers invented nightmares about the catastrophic potential of everything their children did or came in contact with or if she was the one who'd been a closet neurotic, and having Leo had only uncovered her condition.

Even though she was unable to see him clearly in the dark, his every pore and eyelash were engraved in her mind. If anyone had suspected she'd been with Maksim, they would have realized at once that Leo was his son. He was his replica after all. Just like Alex was Aristedes's. When she'd first set eyes on Alex, she *had* exclaimed that cloning had been achieved. Now their daughter Sofia was the spitting image of Selene.

Every day made Leo the baby version of his impossibly beautiful father. His hair had the same unique shade of glossy mahogany, with the same widow's peak, and would no doubt develop the same relaxed wave and luxury. His chin had the same cleft, his left cheek the same dimple. In Maksim's case, since he'd appeared to be incapable of smiling, that dimple had winked at her only in grimaces of agonized pleasure at the height of passion.

The only difference between father and son was the eyes. Though Leo's had the same wolfish slant, it was as if he'd mixed her blue eyes and Maksim's golden ones together in the most amazing shade of translucent olive green.

Feeling her heart expanding with gratitude for this perfect miracle, she bent and touched her lips to Leo's plump downy cheek. He gurgled contentedly and then flounced to his side, stretching noisily before settling into an even sounder sleep. She planted one more kiss over his averted face before finally straightening and walking out.

Closing the door behind her, she leaned against it. But instead of the familiar depression, something new crept in to close its freezing fingers around her heart. Rage. At herself.

Why had she given Maksim the opportunity to be the one to walk out on her? How had she been that weak?

She *had* felt his withdrawal. So why had she clung to him instead of doing what she herself had stipulated from the very beginning? That if the fire weakened or went out, they'd end it, without attempts to prolong its dying throes?

But in her defense, he'd confused her, giving her hope her doubts and observations of his distance had all been in her mind, when after each withdrawal he'd come back hungrier.

Still, that *had* been erratic, and it should have convinced her put a stop to it.

But she'd snatched at his offer to be there for her, even in that impersonal and peripheral way of his, had clung to him even through the dizzying fluctuation of his behavior. She'd given him the chance to deal her the blow of his abrupt desertion. Which she now had to face she hadn't gotten over, and might never recover from.

Rage swerved inside her like a stream of lava to pour over him, burning him, too, in the vehemence of her contempt.

Why had he offered what he'd had no intention of honoring? When she'd assured him she hadn't considered it his obligation? But he'd done worse than renege on his promise. Once he'd had enough of her, he'd begrudged her even the consideration of a goodbye.

Not that she'd understood, *or* believed that he had actually deserted her at the time.

Believing there must be another explanation, she'd started attempting to contact him just a day after his disappearance,

The number he'd assigned her had been disconnected. His other numbers had rung without going to voice mail. Her emails had gone unanswered. None of his associates had known anything about him. Apart from his acquisitions and takeovers, there'd been no other evidence of his continued existence. It had all pointed to the simple, irrefutable truth: he'd gone to serious lengths to hide his high profile, to make it impossible for her to contact him.

Yet for months she hadn't been able to sanction that verdict. She'd grown frantic with every failure, even when logic had said nothing serious could happen to him without the whole world knowing. But, self-deluding fool that she was, she'd been convinced something terrible had happened to him, that he wouldn't have abandoned then ignored her like that.

When she'd finally been forced to admit he'd done just that, it had sent her mad wondering…why?

She'd previously rationalized that his episodic withdrawal was due to the fact that her progressing pregnancy was making it too real for him, probably interfering with his pleasure, or even turning him off her.

Her suspicions had faltered when those instances had been interrupted by even-wilder-than-before encounters. But his evasion of her attempts to reach him had forced her to sanction those suspicions as the only explanation. Then, to make things worse, the deepening misery of her pregnancy's last stages had forced another admission on her.

It hadn't been anguish, or addiction, or needing closure.

She'd fallen in love with Maksim.

When she'd faced that fact, she'd finally known why he'd left. He must have sensed the change in her before she'd become conscious of it, had considered it the breaking point. Because *he'd* never change.

But if she'd thought the last months of her pregnancy had been hellish, they'd been nothing compared to what had followed Leo's birth. To everyone else, she'd functioned perfectly. Inside, no matter what she'd told herself— that she had a perfect baby, a great career, good health, a loving family and financial stability—she'd known true desolation.

It hadn't been the overwhelming responsibility for a helpless being who depended on her every single second of the day. It had been that soul-gnawing longing to have Maksim there with her, to turn to him for counsel, for moral support. She'd needed to *share* Leo with him, the little things more than the big stuff. She'd needed to exclaim to him over Leo's every little wonder, to ramble on about his latest words or actions or a hundred other expected or unique developments. Sharing that with anyone who wasn't Maksim had intensified her yearning for him.

Her condition had worsened until she'd started feeling as if he was near, as if she'd turn to find him looking at her with that uncontainable passion in his eyes. Many times she'd even thought she'd caught glimpses of him, her imagination playing havoc with her mind. And each time this mirage had dissolved, it had been as if he'd walked out on her all over again. Those phantom sensations, that need that wouldn't subside, had only made her more bereft.

Now all that only poured fuel on her newfound fury.

But anger felt far better than despondence. It made her feel alive. She hadn't felt anywhere near that since he'd left.

She was done feeling numb inside. She'd no longer pretend to be alive. She'd live again for real, and to hell with everything she...

The bell rang.

Her heart blipped as her eyes flew to the wall clock. 10 p.m. She couldn't imagine who it could be at this hour. Besides, anyone who came to see her would have buzzed her on the intercom, or, at the very least, her concierge would have called ahead to check with her first. So how could someone just arrive unannounced at her door?

The only answer was Kassandra. Maybe she'd left something behind. Probably her phone, since she hadn't called ahead.

She rushed to the door, opened it without checking the peephole...and everything screeched to a halt.

Her breath. Her heart. The whole world.

In the subdued lights of the spacious corridor he loomed, dark and huge, his face eclipsed by the door's shadow, his eyes glowing gold in the gloom.

Maksim.

Inside the cessation, a maelstrom churned, scrambling her senses. Heartbeats boomed in her chest. Air clogged in her lungs. Had she been thinking of him so obsessively she'd conjured him up? As she'd done so many times before?

Her vision distorted over the face that was omnipresent in her memory. It was the same, yet almost unrecognizable. She couldn't begin to tell why. Her consciousness was wavering and only one thing kept her erect. The intensity of his gaze.

Then something hit her even harder. The way he sagged against the door frame, as if he, too, was unable to stand straight, as enervated at her sight as she was at his. His eyes roamed feverishly over her face, down her body, making her feel he'd scraped all her nerve endings raw.

Then his painstakingly sculpted lips twitched, as if in… pain. Next second it was her who almost fell to the ground in a heap.

The dark, evocative melody that emanated from his lips swamped her. But it was his ragged words that hit her hardest, deepened her paralysis, her muteness.

"Ya ocheen skoocha po tebyeh, moya dorogoya."

She'd been learning Russian avidly since the day she'd met him. She hadn't even stopped after he'd left, had only taken a break when Leo was born. She'd resumed her lessons in the past three months. Why exactly she'd been so committed, she hadn't been able to rationalize. It was just one more thing that was beyond her.

But…maybe she'd been learning for this moment. So she'd understand what he'd just said.

I missed you so terribly, my darling.

Two

That was it. Her mind had snapped.

She was not only seeing Maksim, she was hearing him say the words that had echoed in her head so many times, waking up from a dream where he'd said just that. Then, to complete the hallucination, he reached for her and pulled her into his arms as he'd always done in those tormenting visions.

But he didn't surround her in that sure flow of her dreams, or the steady purpose of the past. He staggered as he groped for her. His uncharacteristic incoordination, the desperation in his vibe, in every inch that impacted her quivering flesh, sent her ever-simmering desire roaring.

Then she was mingled with him, sharing his breath, sinking in his taste, as he reclaimed her from the void he'd plunged her in, wrenching her back into his possession.

Maksim. He was back like she'd dreamed every night for one bleak, interminable year. He was back...*for real*.

But he couldn't be. He'd never been with her for real. It had never become real to him. She'd accepted that in the past.

She wouldn't accept that anymore. Couldn't bear it.

No matter how she'd fantasized about taking him back a thousand times, that would remain an impossible yearning. Too much had changed. She had. And he'd told her he never would.

The fugue of drugging pleasure, of drowning reprieve, slowly lifted. Instead of a resurrection, the feel of him around her became suffocation, until she was struggling for breath.

He let her go at once, stumbled back across her threshold. "*Izvinityeh*... Forgive me.... I didn't mean to..."

His apology choked as he ran both hands through hair that had grown down to the base of his neck. One of the changes that hadn't registered at first that now cascaded into her awareness like dominos, each one knocking a memorized nuance of him, replacing it with his reality now.

He looked...haggard, a shadow of the formidably vital man he'd once been. And, if possible, she found him even more breathtaking for it. That harsh edge of...depletion made her want to crush against him until she assimilated him into her being....

God... Was she turning into her mother for real? Is this the pattern she'd establish now? He'd leave without a word, stay away through her most trying times then come back, and without a word of explanation, say he'd missed her and one soul-stealing kiss later, she'd breathlessly offer him said soul if only he'd take it?

No way. He'd submerged her mind because he'd taken her by surprise, just when he'd been dominating her thoughts. But this lapse wouldn't be repeated.

Maksim was part of her past. And that was where she'd keep him.

Yet even with this resolution, she could only stare up at him as he brooded at her from his prodigious height, what was amplified now by his weight loss.

"Won't you invite me in?"

His rough whisper lashed through her, made her breath leave her in a hiss. "No. And before you leave, I want to know how you made it up here in the first place. Did you con a tenant to let you in, or did you intimidate my concierge?"

He winced. No doubt at the shrill edge in her voice. "I won't say these things are beyond me if I wanted something bad enough. And I certainly would have resorted to whatever would have gotten me up here. But in this case, I didn't have to con or coerce anyone to get my way. I entered with your pass code."

How did he know that?

She'd once thought it remarkable a man of his stature walked around without bodyguards and let her into his inner sanctum without any safeguards. She'd thought he'd trusted her that much.

But what if she'd been wrong about that, too? Had he just seemed trusting because his security measures were of such a caliber they'd been invisible to her senses?

It made sense his security machine dissected anyone with whom he came in contact, especially women with whom he became sexually intimate. Come to think of it, they probably collected evidence on his conquests to be used if they stepped out of line. He probably had a dossier on her every private detail down to the brand of deodorant she used. What if he...

"I once came here with you."

His subdued statement aborted her feverish projections. She stared up at him, unable to fathom the correlation.

"You inputted your pass code at the entrance."

If anything, that explanation left her more stunned. "You mean you watched me as I entered it, and not only figured out the twelve-digit code, but memorized it? Till now?"

He nodded, impatient to leave this behind. "I remember everything about you. Everything, Caliope."

With this emphasis, his gaze dropped to her lips, as if he was holding back from ravishing them with a resolve that was fast dwindling.

Her lips throbbed in response, her insides twitched…

He took a tight step, still not crossing the threshold. Which really surprised her. The Maksim she knew would have just overridden her, secure that he'd melt any resistance. Not that he'd ever met with that, or even the slightest hint of reluctance, from her. But that had been in another life.

"Invite me in, Caliope. I need to talk to you."

"And I don't want to talk to you," she shot back, struggling not to let that…vulnerability in his demand affect her. "You're a year too late. The time for talking was before you decided to leave without a word. I got over any need or willingness to talk to you nine months ago."

His nod was difficult. "When Leonid was born."

So he knew Leo's name, though he used the Russian version of Leonidas. He probably also knew Leo's weight and how many baby teeth he had. All part of that security dossier he must have on her.

"Your deduction is redundant. As is your presence here."

His hands bunched and released, as if they itched. "I won't say I deserve that you hear me out. But for months you did want to hear my explanation of my sudden departure. You wanted to so badly, you left me dozens of messages and as many emails."

So he had ignored her, let her go mad worrying, as she'd surmised. "Since you remember everything, you must remember why I kept calling and emailing."

"You wanted to know if I was okay."

"And since I can see that you are…" She paused, looked him up and down in his long, dark coat. "Though maybe I can't call what you are now *okay*. You look like a starving vampire who is trying to hypnotize his victim into letting him in so he can suck her dry. Or for a more mundane metaphor, you look as if you've developed a cocaine habit."

She knew she was being cruel. But she couldn't help it. He'd sprung back into her life after bitterness had swept away despondence and anger had cracked its floodgates. Feeling herself about to throw all her anguish to the wind and just drag him in after one kiss had brought the dam of resentment crashing down.

"I've been…ill."

The reluctant way he said that, the way his eyes lowered and those thick, thick lashes touched his even more razor-sharp cheekbones made her heart overturn again in her chest.

What if he'd been ill all this time…?

No. She wasn't doing what her mother had done with her father—making excuses for him until he destroyed her.

He raised his gaze to her. "Aren't you even curious to know why I left? Why I'm back?"

Curious? Speculating on why he'd left had permanently eroded her sanity. Her brain was now expanding inside her head with the pressure of needing to know why he was back.

Out loud she said, "No, I'm not. I made a deal with you from day one, demanding only two things from you. Honesty and respect. But you weren't honest about having had enough of me, and you would have shown someone you'd picked off the street more respect."

He flinched as if she'd struck him but didn't make any attempt to interrupt her.

It only brought back more of memories of her anguish, injected more harshness into her words. "You evaded me as you would a stalker, when you knew that if you'd only confirmed that you were okay, I would have stopped calling. I did stop when your news made the confirmation for you, forcing me to believe the depth of your mistreatment. You've forfeited any right to my consideration. I don't care why you left, why you ignored me, and I don't have the least desire to know why you're back."

His bleakness deepened with her every word. When he was sure her barrage was over, he exhaled raggedly. "None of what you just said has any basis in truth. And while you might never sanction my true reasons for behaving as I did, they were…overwhelming to me at the time. It's a long story." Before she could blurt out that she wasn't interested in hearing it, he added, almost inaudibly, "Then I was…in an accident."

That silenced her. Outwardly. Inside, a cacophony of questions, anxiety and remorse exploded.

When? How? What happened? Was he injured? How badly?

Her eyes darted over him, feverishly inspecting him for damage. She saw nothing on his face, but maybe she was missing scars in the dimness. What about his body? That dark shroud might not obscure that he'd lost a lot of his previous bulk, but what if it was covering up something far more horrific?

Unable to bear the questions, she grabbed his forearm and dragged him across the threshold, where the better lighting of her foyer made it possible for her to check him closely.

Her heart squeezed painfully. God… He'd lost so much weight, looked so…unwell, gaunt, almost…frail.

Suddenly he groaned and dropped down. Before fright could register, he rose again, scooping her up in his arms.

It was a testament to his strength that, even in his diminished state, he could do so with seeming effortlessness, making her feel as he always had whenever he'd carried her: weightless, taken, coveted, cosseted. The blow of longing, the sense of homecoming when she'd despaired of ever seeing him again, was so overpowering it had her sagging in his hold, all tension and resistance gone.

Her head rolled over his shoulder, her hands trembled in a cold tangle over his chest as all the times he'd had her in his arms like this flooded her memory. He'd always carried her, had told her he loved the feel of her filling his arms, relinquishing her weight and will to him, so he'd contain her, take her, wherever and however he would.

He stopped at her family room. If she could have found her voice, she would have told him to keep going to her room, to not stop until they were flesh to flesh, ending the need for words, letting her lose herself in his possession, and even more, reassure herself about his every inch, check it out against what she remembered in obsessive detail, yearned for in perpetual craving.

But he was setting her down on the couch, kneeling on the ground beside her, looking down at her as she lay back, unable to muster enough power to sit up. And that was before she saw something…enormous roiling in his eyes.

Then he articulated it. "Can I see Leonid?"

Everything in her, body and spirit, stiffened with shock. All she could say was, "Why?"

She was asking in earnest. He'd told her he wouldn't take any personal interest or part in Leo's life. She could find no reason why he would want to see him now.

His answer put into words what she'd just thought. "I know I said I wouldn't have anything to do with him personally. But it wasn't because I didn't want to. It was because I thought I couldn't and mustn't."

The memory of those excruciating moments, when she'd accepted that he'd never be part of the radical change that would forever alter her life's course, assailed her again with the immediacy of a fresh injury.

"You said you're not 'a man to be trusted in such situations.'"

A spasm seized his face. "You remember."

Instead of saying she remembered everything about him, as he claimed to about her, she exhaled. "That was kind of impossible to forget."

"I only said that because I believed it was in your and his best interest not to have me in your lives."

"Is the reason you believed that part of the…long story?"

"The reason *is* the story. But before I go into it, will you please let me see Leonid?"

God… He'd asked again. This was really happening. He was here and he wanted to see Leo. But if she let him, nothing would ever be the same again. She just knew it wouldn't.

She groped for any excuse to stop this from spiraling any further. "He's asleep…."

His eclipsed eyes darkened even more. "I promise I will just look at him, won't disturb his sleep."

She tried again. "You won't see much in the dark. And I can't turn the lights on. It's the only thing that wakes him up."

"Even if I can't see him well, I will…feel him. I already know what he looks like."

Her heart lurched. Had she been right about this security report? "How do you know? Are you having us followed?"

He stared at her for a moment as if he didn't understand. "Why would you even think that?"

Regarding him warily, she told him all her suspicions. His frown deepened with every word. "You have every right to believe the worst of me. But I never invaded your privacy. If I ever were to have you followed, it would be for your protection, not mine. And I had no reason to fear for your safety before, since associating with me would have been the only source of danger to you, and I kept our relationship a firm secret."

"So how do you know what Leo looks like?"

"Because *I* followed you."

Her mouth dropped open. "You did? When?"

He bit his lip, words seeming to hurt as he forced them out. "On and off. Mostly on for the past three months."

So she hadn't been imagining it or going insane! All the times she'd felt him, he had been there!

Questions and confusions deluged her. Why had he done that? Why had he slipped away the moment she'd felt him? Why hadn't he approached her? And why had he decided to finally do so now? Why, why, *why?*

She wanted to bombard him with every why and how could you, to have answers *now,* not a second later.

But those answers would take time. And though she might be her mother's daughter after all, she couldn't press him for them now. She couldn't deny him access to his son. Even without explanations, the beseeching in his eyes told her enough. He'd waited too long already.

She nodded, tried to sit up and pressed into him when he didn't move. His hands shot out to support her when she almost collapsed back, his eyes glazing as that electricity that always flowed between them zapped them both.

As if he were unable to stop, his hand cupped her cheek, slid around her nape, tilting her face up to his. He groaned her name as if in pain, as if warning her he'd kiss her if she didn't say no. She didn't. She couldn't.

As if she'd removed a barbed leash from his neck, relief rumbled from his depths as he lowered his head, took her lips in a compulsive kiss.

She knew she shouldn't let this happen again, that nothing had been resolved and never would be. But at the glide of his tongue against hers, the mingling of his breath with hers, she was, as always, lost.

She surrendered to his hunger as his lips and teeth plucked at her trembling flesh, as his tongue plunged into her mouth, plundering her response. Her body melted, readied itself for him, remembering his invasion, his dominance, his pleasures, weeping for it all. He pressed her back on the couch and bore down on her, restlessly moving against her, rubbing her swollen breasts and aching nipples with the hardness of his chest... Then, without warning, he suddenly wrenched his lips from hers, shot up on his knees, his eyes wide in alarm.

It took her hard-breathing moments to realize the whimper she'd heard hadn't come from her. *Leo.*

It took a few more gurgles for her to remember the baby monitor. She had a unit in every room.

This time when she struggled up, Maksim helped her. She didn't know if his hands were shaking or if hers were, or both.

He rose to his feet, helped her to hers then stood aside so she'd lead the way.

The unreality of the situation swamped her again as she approached Leo's room, feeling Maksim's presence flooding her apartment. The last thing she'd imagined when she'd last made that same trip was that in an hour's time, Maksim would be here and she'd be taking him for his first contact with her... With his... With *their* son.

She felt his tension increase with every step until she opened the door, and it almost knocked her off her feet.

She turned to him. "Relax, okay? Leo is very sensitive

to moods." It was why he'd given her a hellish first six months. He'd been responding to her misery. She'd managed to siphon it into a grueling exercise and work schedule, and to compartmentalize her emotions so she didn't expose him to their negative side. "If he wakes, you don't want him seeing you for the first time with this intensity coming off you."

She almost groaned. She'd said "the first time" as if she thought this encounter would be the first of many. When Maksim probably only wanted to see him once because… She had no idea why.

Unaware of her turmoil, grappling with his, he squeezed his eyes shut before opening them again and nodding. "I'm ready."

Nerves jangling, she tiptoed into the room with him soundlessly following her. She hoped Leo had settled down. She really preferred this first, and probably last, sighting to happen while he was asleep. The next moment, tension drained as she found Leo snoring gently again.

Before she could sigh in relief, everything disappeared from her awareness, even Leo, as Maksim came to stand beside her. Adapting to the dark room, she stared at his profile, her heart rattling inside her chest like a coin in a box. She'd never imagined he would…would… God.

His expression, the searing emotion that emanated from him as he looked down at Leo… It stormed through her, brought tears surging from her depths to fill eyes she'd thought had dried forever.

His face was a mask of stunned, sublime…suffering, as if he were gazing down at a heart that had spilled out of his chest and taken human form. As if he were beholding a miracle.

Which Leo was. Against all odds, he'd come into being.

And with all she'd suffered since she'd seen the evidence
of his existence, she would never have it any other way.

"Can—can I touch him?"

The reverent whisper almost felled her.

He swung his gaze to her and she nearly cried out. His
eyes! Glittering in the faint light…with tears.

Tears? Maksim? How was that even possible?

Feeling her heart in her throat, she could only nod.

After hard-breathing moments when he seemed to be
bracing himself, he reached a trembling hand down to
Leo's face.

The moment his fingertips touched Leo's averted cheek,
his inhalation was so sharp, it was as if he'd been punched
in the gut. It was how she felt, too, as if her lungs had
emptied and wouldn't fill again. And that was before Leo
pressed his cheek into Maksim's large hand, like a cat demanding a firmer petting.

Swaying visibly now, or maybe it was her world that
was, Maksim complied, cupping Leo's plump, downy
cheek, caressing it with his thumb, over and over, his
breathing erratic and audible now, as if he'd just sprinted
a mile.

"Are all children this amazing?"

His ragged words were so thick, so low, and not only
on account of not wanting to disturb Leo. It seemed he
could barely speak. And his words weren't an exclamation of wonder or a rhetorical question. He was asking for
real. He truly had no idea. It was as if it was the first time
he'd seen a child, at least the first time he'd realized how
incredible it was for a human being to be so tiny yet so
compact and complete, so precious and perfect. So frag-
ile and dependent, yet so overpowering.

She considered not answering him. The lump in her
throat was about to dissolve into fractured sobs at any

moment. But she couldn't ignore his question, not when his gleaming eyes beseeched her answers.

Mustering all she had so she wouldn't break down, she whispered, "All children are. But it seems we are equipped with this affinity to our own, this bond that makes us appreciate them more than anything else in the world, that amplifies their assets, downplays their disadvantages and makes us withstand their trials and tribulations with an endurance that's virtually unending and unreasoning."

His expression was rapt as he listened to her, as if every word was a revelation to him. But suddenly his face shut down. The change was jarring, and that was before his rumble repeated her last word, reverberating inside her, fierce, almost scary.

"Unreasoning..."

Before she could say or think anything, he looked down at Leo for one last moment, withdrew his hand and stalked out of the room.

She followed, slowly, her mind in an uproar.

What was up with this confounding, maddening man?

What did he mean by all that? Coming here, the unprecedented show of emotions for her, that soul-shaking reaction at seeing Leo up close…and then suddenly this switch to predator-with-a-thorn-in-his-paw mode?

Was this what he'd meant when he'd said he wasn't a man to be trusted "in such situations"? Did he suffer from some bipolar disorder that made him blow hot and cold without rhyme or reason? Did that explain his fluctuations in their last months together? His unexplained desertion and sudden return?

She caught up with him in the living room. He stood waiting for her, his face dark and remote.

She faced him, anger sizzling to the surface again. "I don't know what your problem is, and I don't want to know. You came here uninvited, blindsided me into a couple of kisses and wheedled your way into seeing Leo. And now you're done. I want you to leave and I don't want you to ever come back or I…"

"I come from a family of abusers."

To say his out-of-the-blue statement flabbergasted her would be like saying that Mount Everest was a molehill.

Her mind emptied. There was just nothing possible to think—or to say—to what he'd just stated.

He went on, in that same inanimate voice. "It probably goes back to the beginnings of my lineage, but I only know for a fact that my great-grandfather was one, and that the disorder got worse with every generation, reaching its most violent level with my father. I believed it ran in my blood, that once I manifested it, I would be the worst of them all. That was why I never considered having any relationship. Until you."

She could only stare at him, quakes starting in her very essence, spreading outward. She'd lived for a year going crazy for an explanation. Now she no longer wanted to know. Not if the explanation was worse than his seeming desertion itself.

But she couldn't find her voice to tell him to stop. Not that he would have stopped. He seemed set on getting this out in the open once and for all.

"From that first moment," he said, his voice a throb of melancholy, "I wanted you with a ferocity that terrified me, so when you stipulated the finite, uninvolved nature of our liaison, I was relieved. I believed it would be safe as long as our involvement was temporary, remained superficial. But things didn't go as expected, and my worry intensified along with my hunger for you. I lived in fear of my reaction if you wanted to walk away when I wasn't ready to let go. But instead, you became pregnant."

She continued to stare helplessly at him, legs starting to quiver, feeling he hadn't told her the worst of it yet.

He proved her right. "As you blossomed with Leonid, I was more certain every day I'd been right to tell you I'd withdraw from your life eventually and never enter his. I found myself inventing anxieties every second you were out of my sight, had to constantly struggle to curb my impulses so I wouldn't smother you. I even tried to stay away from you as much as I could bear it. But I only returned even hungrier, feared it would only be a matter of time before all these unprecedented emotions snapped my control and manifested in aggression. That was why I forced myself to leave you before you had Leo. Before I ended up doing what my father did after my sister was born."

He had a sister?

His next words provided a horrific answer to her unvoiced surprise. "He'd been getting progressively more volatile. There were no longer days when he didn't hit my mother or me or both of us. Then one night, when Ana was about six months old, he went berserk. He put us all in the emergency room that night. It took my mother and I months to get over our injuries. Ana struggled for a week before she…succumbed."

Three

Maksim's words fell on Cali like an avalanche of rocks.

She stood gaping at him, buried under their enormity.

His father had killed his sister. His baby *sister.*

He feared he suffered from the same brutal affliction.

Was that what had overcome him back there in Leo's room? This "unreasoning" aggression toward the helpless?

Sudden terror grabbed her by the throat.

What if he lost control now? What if— What if…

As suddenly as dread had towered, it crashed, deflated.

This man standing across her living room, looking at her with eyes that bled with despondence she recognized only too well, having suffered it for far too long, wasn't in the grips of uncontrollable violence. But of overwhelming anguish.

He feared himself and what he considered to be his legacy. That fear seemed to have ruled his whole life. He'd just finished telling her it had dictated his every action and decision in his interactions with her. The limits he'd agreed to, the severance he'd imposed on them, had been prodded by nothing else. He'd thought he was protecting her, and Leo, from his destructive potential.

And she heard herself asking, "Did you ever hurt anyone?"

"I did."

The bitten-off admission should have resurrected her fears. It didn't. And not because she was seeing good where there was none, as her mother had done with her father. As his own mother must have done with his father, to remain with an abusive husband.

She only couldn't ignore her gut feeling. It had guided her all her life, had never led her astray.

The one time she'd thought she'd made a fundamental mistake had been with him. But his explanations had reinstated the validity of her inner instincts about him.

From the first moment she'd laid eyes on Maksim, she'd felt she'd be safe with him. More. Protected, defended. At any cost to him. That nobility, that stability, that perfect control she'd felt from him—even at the height of passion—had led her to trust him without reservation from that first night onward. It all contradicted what he feared about himself.

She started walking toward him and he tensed. It was clear he didn't welcome her nearness now, after he'd confessed his shame and dread to her. What must it be like for him to doubt himself on such a basic level? What had it been like for him believing he had a time bomb ticking inside him?

She had to let him know what she'd always sensed of his steadiness and trustworthiness. That it had been why it had hit her so hard when he'd left. She hadn't been able to reconcile what she'd felt on her most essential levels with his seemingly callous actions. Thinking she'd been so wrong about him had agonized her as much as longing for him had.

But she'd been right about him. As misguided as his reasons had been, he'd only meant to protect her and Leo.

He took a couple of steps back as she approached, his eyes imploring her not to come any closer, not just yet.

"Let me say this. It's been weighing on me since I met you. But if you come near me, I'll forget everything."

In answer, she stopped, sank down on the couch where he'd ravished her with pleasure so recently and patted the space next to her. He reluctantly complied.

"Those you hurt were never weaker than you are." It was a statement, not a question.

His hooded eyes simmered. "No."

"They were equals…" her gaze darted over the daunting breadth of his shoulders "…or superior numbers." His nod was terse, confirming her deduction. "And you never instigated violence."

"But I didn't only ward off attacks or defend the attacked. I was only appeased when I damaged the attackers."

"Were those times so frequent?"

He nodded. "My father left another legacy. A tangled mess in our home city. In the motherland, some areas are far from the jurisdiction of law, or the law leaves certain disputes to be resolved by people among themselves. The use of force is the most accepted resolution. I became an expert at it."

"So those times you hurt others, you were not only defending yourself but others. You did what had to be done."

"I was too violent. And I relished it."

She persisted. "Did you lose control?"

"No. I knew exactly what I was doing."

"A lot of men are like you…. Soldiers, protectors—capable of stunning violence, of even killing, for a cause, to defend others against aggressors. But those same men are usually the gentlest men with those who depend on them for protection."

His eyes grew more turbid. "I understood that mentally, that I had good cause. But with my family history, I feared it meant I had it in me…this potential for unprovoked vio-

lence. My passion for you was intensifying by the hour…
but my fear of myself came to a head one specific night.
It happened when I was waiting for you in bed and you
were walking toward me in a sheer turquoise negligee."

Her throat closed. She remembered that night. Only too
well. Their last night together.

She'd woken up replete from his tender, tempestuous
lovemaking to find him gone.

"I'd never seen you more beautiful. You were ripe and
glowing—your belly was rounding more by the day, and
you were stroking it lovingly as you approached me. What
I felt at that moment, it was so ferocious, I was scared out
of my wits. I'd put bullies twice your size in traction…or
worse. I couldn't risk having my passions swerve into a
different direction."

Needles pricked behind her eyes, threatening to dissolve down her cheeks at any moment. "You hid it well."

His eyes widened in dismay. "I didn't have to hide
anything. I never felt anything anywhere near aggressive
around you. But the mere possibility of losing control of
my passion carried a price that was impossible to contemplate."

He never said emotion. Did he use passion interchange-
ably, or was everything he felt rooted in the physical?

"You have to believe me. You don't have to look back
and feel sick thinking you'd been in danger and oblivious of it."

She shook her head, needing to arrest his alarm. "I
meant you hid that increasing passion. I never sensed that
you felt a different level from what you had always showed
me."

His nod was heavy. "*That* I hid. And the more I tried not
to show you what I felt, the more it…roiled inside me. And

if I felt like this when you were still carrying my child, I couldn't risk testing how I'd feel after you had him."

He must have been living a nightmare, worrying he'd relive what had happened with his father, reenact it.

A vice clamped her throat. "Abusers don't fear for their victims' well-being, Maksim. They blame them for provoking them, make themselves out to be the wronged ones, the ones pushed beyond their endurance. They certainly don't live in dread of what they might do. You're nothing like your father."

The pain gripping his face twisted her vitals. "I couldn't be certain, couldn't risk a margin of error."

"Tell me about him."

He inhaled sharply, as if he hadn't expected that request, as if he loathed talking about his father.

He still nodded, complied. "He was possessive of my mother to madness, insanely jealous of the air she breathed, suspicious of her every move. He begrudged her each moment alone or with anyone else. It got so bad he went into rages at the attention she bestowed on his children. Then came the day he convinced himself she was neglecting him on our account, because we weren't his."

"And that was when he...he..."

He nodded. "After he beat us to a pulp, he rushed us to emergency. On the day he was told my sister was dead, he walked out onto the street and let himself be run over by a truck."

God, the sheer horror and sickness, the magnitude of damage was...unimaginable. How had his mother survived, first sustaining the brunt of her husband's violence then suffering such an incalculable loss because of it? Had she survived? At least emotionally, psychologically? How could she have?

She finally whispered, "How—how old were you then?"

"Nine."

Old enough to understand fully, to be scarred permanently. And to have suffered intensely for far too long.

"And you've since been afraid you'd turn into him."

His eyes loathed the very thought that he might be so horrifically infected. She stopped herself from reaching a soothing hand to his cheek. Not yet. It wouldn't stop at a touch this time. And he needed to get this off his chest.

"Your mother didn't realize he was unstable before she married him?"

The loathing turned on the father who'd blighted his existence. "She admitted she'd seen signs of it while he was courting her. But she was young and poor and he was a larger-than-life entity whose pursuit swept her off her feet. She did realize he was disturbed the first time he knocked her down. But he was always so distraught, so loving afterward, that she kept sinking deeper into the trap of his diseased passion. It was a mess, a never-ending circle of fear and abuse. Then came Ana's unforeseen pregnancy."

Like hers, with Leo. Yet another parallel that must have poured fuel on his untenable projections.

"She thought of aborting her, terrified her pregnancy would trigger a new level of instability, as it did. The best thing he ever did was step in front of that truck, ridding her of his existence. But after all the harm he'd inflicted, it was too little, too late."

It was unthinkable what his father had cost them.

But… "Stepping in front of that truck might have rid her of his physical danger, but that he seemingly forfeited his life to atone for his sins must have robbed her of the closure that hating him unequivocally could have brought her."

His eyes widened as if she'd slapped him awake. "I thought I dissected this subject, and him, to death a million times already. But this is a perspective I never considered. You could be right. *Bozhe moy*...you probably are. That bastard. Even dying, he still managed to torture her."

There was no doubt Maksim loved his mother, felt ferociously protective of her. Would defend her to the death without a second thought. And this, to her, was more proof that he'd always been wrong to fear himself.

"But why did you even think you'd one day develop into another version of him? When you hate what he was so profoundly?"

"Because I thought hating something didn't necessarily mean I wouldn't become it. And the evidence of three generations of Volkov men was just too horrifically compelling. I learned about them later on, so they had no impact on shaping my life. I made my decision never to become involved with anyone that night Ana died. I didn't question my resolve for the next thirty years, never felt the need to be close to anyone. Then came you."

The way he kept saying this. *Until you. Then came you.* As if she'd changed his life. As if...he loved her?

No. He was being totally honest, and if this was how he felt, he would have confessed it.

"I left, determined to never come back, even when all I wanted was to stay with you...to be the first to hold Leonid, to be there every single second from then on for you and him. But I couldn't abide by the sentence I imposed on myself. I started following you, like an addict would the only thing that could quench his addiction. I had to see that you and Leonid were all right, to be near enough to step in if you ever needed me."

We needed you—I needed you every second of the past year.

But she couldn't say this. Not yet.

For now, he'd answered the questions that had been burning in her mind and soul. All that remained was one.

"What made you show yourself now, after you slipped away for months whenever I noticed you?"

This seemed to shock him. "You did? I thought I made sure you wouldn't."

"I still did. I…felt you."

The bleakness of dwelling on the tragic past evaporated in a blast of passion. She'd barely absorbed this radical switch when he singed her hands in the heat of his hands and lips.

Before she threw herself in his arms, come what may, he captured her face in his hands, the tremor in them transmitting to her whole body like a quake.

"That deal we made our first night," he groaned against her trembling flesh, "and the one I made when you told me you were pregnant with Leonid…"

A thunderclap went off in her chest. He wanted to reinstate them?

"I want to strike new deals. I want to be Leonid's father for real, in every way—and your husband."

Maksim watched stupefaction spread like wildfire over Caliope's exquisite face.

Bozhe moy…how he'd missed that face. The face sculpted from the shape of his every taste and desire, every angle and dimple the very embodiment of elegance, harmony and intelligence. How he'd longed for every lash and fleck of those bluer-than-heaven eyes, every strand of this dipped-in-gold caramel hair, how he'd yearned for every inch of that sun-infused skin and that made-for-passion body. And then came every spark of her being— every glance, every breath, her scent, her feel, her hunger.

His gaze and senses devoured it all, his starvation only

intensifying the more he took in. It wasn't only because he'd been deprived of her, or was maddened by the taste he'd just gotten of her ecstasy. He'd felt constantly famished even when he'd been gorging himself on all that she was.

It was why he'd distrusted himself so much, feared the intensity of his need. But everything had changed. He had.

As if coming out of a trance, Caliope blinked, then opened her lips. Nothing came.

His proposal had shocked her that much. Though her reaction was the only one he'd expected, it still twisted the knife he'd embedded in his own guts when he'd walked away from her.

She tried again, produced a wavering whisper. "You want to marry…" She stopped as if she couldn't say *marry me*. "You want to get married?"

He nodded, his heart crowding with too much.

Her throat worked, as if this was too big a lump for her to swallow. "Sorry if I can't process this, especially after what you just told me. What could have changed your mind so diametrically?" Suddenly those azure eyes that he saw in his every waking and sleeping moment widened. "Is this because of the accident you had? Has it changed your perspective?"

He could only nod again.

"Will you tell me what happened? Or will it take years before you're ready to talk about it, too?"

Unable to sit beside her anymore without taking her into his arms, he heaved himself up to his feet. He knew he had to tell her what she had a right to know. She stared up at him, a hundred dizzying emotions fast-forwarding on her face.

He braced himself against the temptation to sink back

over her, convince her to forget everything now, just let him give them the assuagement they were both dying for.

He balled itching hands, smothering the need to fill them with her. "I'm here to offer you full disclosure."

She sagged back against the couch, as if she felt she'd be unable to take the rest of his confessions unsupported.

He wanted to start, but found no way to put the emptiness and loss inside him into words.

"Don't look for a way to tell me. Just…tell me."

Her quiet words surprised him so much his heart faltered.

Despite their tempestuous passion, he'd never felt they'd shared anything…emotional, psychological, let alone spiritual. He'd wondered if it had been because of their pact of noninvolvement, or if there was simply nothing between them beyond that addicting, unstoppable chemistry.

But she'd felt his inability to contain his ordeal into expression, his struggle to find a way that would be less traumatic than what it had been in truth.

Had she always possessed this ability to read him, but hadn't employed it—or at least shown it— because it had been against their agreement? Or had he hidden his feelings too well, as she'd said, and succeeding in blocking her? Had she ever wished to come closer? If she had, why hadn't she demanded a change in the terms of their involvement? Or was she only now reaching out to him on a human, not intimate, level?

This last possibility made the most sense. She *had* shown him understanding he hadn't felt entitled to wish for, had argued his case against his own self-condemnation with reason and conviction. When all he'd hoped for was to make a full confession, to beg for her forgiveness, to ask for any measure of closeness to her and to Leonid that she'd grant.

Not that he'd abided by the humble limitations of his hopes. One glimpse of her and his greed had roared to the forefront. He'd wanted all of her, everything with her.

But now that she hadn't turned him down out of hand, he could dare to hope that an acceptance of his proposal wasn't impossible. But he couldn't press for one. Not now. Not before he told her everything.

He inhaled. "You remember Mikhail?"

She blinked at the superfluous question. For she knew Mikhail well. His only friend, the only one who'd known about him and Caliope.

Whenever they'd gone out with him, he'd felt she'd connected with Mikhail on a level she'd never done with him. He'd felt a twinge of dismay at the…ease they shared. Not jealousy, just disappointment that, in spite of their intense intimacy, this simple connection, this comfortable bond would always be denied them.

But he'd known there'd been no element of attraction. At least on her side. On Mikhail's— What man would not feel a tug in his blood at her overpowering femininity? But being his friend, and more, hers, had been Mikhail's only priority. And though Maksim had felt left out when those two had laughed together, he'd been glad she could share this with his friend when he couldn't offer her the same level of spontaneity.

Caliope's eyes grew wary. "How can I forget him? Though he disappeared from my life the same time you did, I like to think he became my friend, too."

"He did. He was." She lurched at the word *was,* horror flooding her eyes. He forced the agony into words that shredded him on their way out. "He died in the accident."

Her face convulsed as if she'd been stabbed. Then before his burning eyes, the anguish of finality gradually filled hers, overflowing in pale tracks down suddenly flushed cheeks.

He'd once delighted in the sight of her tears. When he'd tormented her with too long anticipation, then devastated her with too much pleasure. Her tears were ones of sorrow now, and those gutted him.

Suddenly confusion invaded her eyes, diluting the shock and grief. "You mean you weren't involved? But you said…"

He gritted his teeth. "I was involved. I survived."

Eyes almost black, she extended her hand to him.

She was reaching out to him, literally, showing him the consideration she'd said she didn't owe him. His chest burned with what felt like melting shards of glass.

Taking her trembling hand made the intimacies he'd taken tonight pale in comparison to that simple voluntary touch. With a ragged exhalation, he sagged down beside her again.

Then he began. "Mikhail was involved in extreme sports." She nodded. She'd known that…and had worried. "When I couldn't dissuade him to stop, I joined him."

Mikhail had left it up to him to tell her he shared his pursuits. He hadn't. The realization of yet another major omission on his part filled her eyes. Another thing he had to answer for.

He forced himself to go on. "I felt better about his stunts sharing them, so I'd be there if something went wrong. For years it seemed nothing could. He was meticulous in his safety measures, and I admit, everything he came up with was freeing and exhilarating. It also intensified our bond when I experienced firsthand what constituted a fundamental part of what made him the man he was. Then one day, during a record-setting skydive, my parachute didn't open."

The sharpness of her inhalation felt as if it had sheared through his own lungs.

Was she unable to bear imagining his peril, or would she have reacted the same to that of anyone?

It was at this moment that he realized. This woman he wanted with every fiber of his being, who had borne his only son... He didn't know her.

Not what affected her emotionally or appealed to her mentally, not what provoked her anger, what inspired her happiness, what commanded her respect.

Right now, her eyes were explicit, overflowing with dread, awaiting the rest of the account of what had changed his life forever...and had written the end of Mikhail's.

He exhaled. "Mikhail swerved to help me. We couldn't both use his parachute like in a tandem dive, as this was a record dive and our parachutes didn't have the necessary clips. We were fast approaching the point where it would be too late to open parachutes, and I kept shouting for him to open his own and I'd manage on my own. He wouldn't comply, forcing me to shove him away. But he dove at me again, grabbed me and opened his parachute."

Her hand convulsed over his. His other hand caressed her, shaking with remembered horror. "The force of the opening chute yanked him away. He miraculously clung to me with his legs, then managed to secure me. But our combined weight made us drop too fast, and we'd strayed far from our intended landing spot over a forest. I knew we'd both die, if not from the drop, then from being shredded falling through those trees. So I struggled away, praying that losing my weight would slow his descent and make him able to maneuver away. I struggled with my parachute one last time and it suddenly opened. It felt as if it was the very next second that I crashed into the top of the trees. Then I knew nothing more."

He stopped, the combined agony of what had come after and her reaction to his account so far an inexorable fist squeezing his throat. Her tears had stopped, but her eyes were horrified, her breath fractured.

He'd thought she'd only felt desire for him. Then when she'd become pregnant, he'd thought an extra dimension had been added to her feelings, what any woman would feel toward the man with whom she shared the elemental bond of a child.

But had she felt…more? Did her reaction mean she still did? How could she, after what he'd done?

The plausible explanation was that she'd react this way to anyone else's ordeal. He shouldn't be reading more into this. And he had to get this torture over with.

"It was dark when I came to. I was disoriented, not to mention in agony. Both my legs were broken—compound fractures, as I learned later—and I was bleeding from injuries all over my body. It took me a while to put together what had happened, and to realize I was stuck high up in a tree. It was so painful to move, I wanted to give up, stay there until I died of exposure. The only thing that kept me trying to climb down was needing to know that Mikhail had made it down safely."

Twin tears escaped from eyes growing more wary, as if she sensed there was much more to this account than just the catastrophic ending he'd told her about upfront.

"My phone was damaged, so I couldn't even hope anyone would follow its GPS signal. I could only hope Mikhail's was working, that he was okay or at least in much better shape than I was. I kept fading in and out of consciousness, and it took me all night to climb half the way down. Then it was light enough…and I saw him in a small clearing dozens of feet away, half covered in his parachute, twisted in such a position it was clear…"

The memory tore into his mind, blasted apart his soul all over again. His throat sealed on the molten lead of agony. And that was before Caliope sobbed and reached for him, hugging him with all her strength.

He surrendered to her solicitude, grateful for it as he felt the tears he hadn't known except when Ana then Mikhail had died, surge to his eyes. He hugged her back, absorbed her shudders into his, feeling her warmth flood his stone-cold being. She didn't prod him to continue, wanted to spare him reliving the details of those harrowing times.

But he wanted to tell her. He couldn't hold any detail or secret from her. Not anymore. He needed her to make a decision based on full disclosure this time.

"I finally made it to his side, but there was nothing I could do for him except keep him warm, keep promising I'd get him through this. But he knew only one of us could walk out of this alive. I'm still enraged that it was me." He inhaled raggedly as she tightened her arms around him. "He confessed he'd directed his parachute toward me, afraid he'd lose me in the forest. He reached me as I hit the trees and twisted us in midfall to take the brunt. He killed himself saving me."

A whimper spilled from her lips as she buried her face in his chest, her tears seeping through his clothes to singe him down to his essence.

"But he didn't die quickly. It was a full day before he… slipped through my fingers. I lay there with him dead in my arms as night fell and day came over and over, praying I'd die, too. I kept losing consciousness, every time think-ing the end had finally come, only to suffer the disappoint-ment of waking up again, finding him in my arms—and feeling as if he'd just died again. It was four more days be-fore his GPS signal was tracked down." Another wrench-ing sob tore out of her, shaking her whole body. He pressed her head harder into his chest, as if to siphon her agitation into his booming heart. "I reached the hospital half-dead, and they spent months putting me back together. The moment I was on my feet again, I came here."

She raised tear-soaked eyes to him. "And followed me and Leo around." He could only nod. She bit her trembling lip. "How—how long ago was the accident?"

"Less than a month after I left."

The hand resting on his biceps squeezed it convulsively. "I knew it. I felt something had happened to you. It was what drove me insane when you didn't answer me. But when I heard you were closing deals, I thought it was only self-delusions."

"My deputies were responsible for the deals, under the tightest secrecy about my condition to guard against widespread panic in my companies or with my shareholders. Though you know now the accident wasn't why I didn't answer you. I intended to never respond, but I kept waiting for your calls, rereading your messages incessantly, compulsively. And the day you stopped…"

His arms tightened around her. He'd been counting the days till her due date, and when she stopped calling, he'd known she'd given birth. Knowing that she and Leonid were fine had been the only thing that had kept his mind in one piece. He'd kept hoping she'd start calling again after a while, at the same time hoping she never would. And she never had. She'd given up on him as he'd prayed she would. Yet it had still destroyed him.

"You kept saying, 'Just let me know if you're okay.' But what could I have told you? 'I'm not? Not physically and not psychologically? And would never be?'"

Her tears stopped as she pulled back to look earnestly into his eyes. "It isn't inevitable the abused became abusers, Maksim. And heredity is not any more certain. You've displayed none of your menfolk's instability, certainly not with me. Why should you believe you'd turn into a monster when the record of your own behavior doesn't support this fear in any way?"

"I couldn't risk it then. But everything has changed."

Contemplation invaded her incredible gemlike eyes. "Because you faced death, and lost your only friend to it? Did that change what you believe about yourself?"

He shook his head. "It wasn't facing my mortality that did it. It was that last day with Mikhail. He told me he didn't risk his life for me only because of what he felt for me as his best friend, but also because I was the one among the two of us who had others who needed me…you and Leonid, and my mother. He made me promise I wouldn't waste any of the life he'd sacrificed himself to save, to live for him, as well as myself. The more I thought of what he said as I recuperated, the more the hatred toward my father, and by extension myself, dissipated. I finally faced that my paralyzing fear wasn't a good enough reason to not reach out to you, the one woman I ever wanted, to the child you've blessed me with. And here I am. But I'll make sure you'll both be safe, from me…and from everything else in the world."

She pulled back in the circle of his arms, eyes stunned.

And he asked again. "Will you take me as your husband and father of your child, *moya dorogoya?* I want to give you and Leonid all of me, everything that I am and have to offer."

Her eyes… *Bozhe moy…* He'd never hoped he'd see such…emotion in them. Was all that for him, or was it maybe relief at the possibility of not being a single parent anymore?

Whatever it was, he hadn't told her everything yet.

He had to. It was the least he owed her.

He caught the hand that trembled up to his cheek, pressed his lips into its palm, feeling he was about to jump out of that plane again, without a parachute at all this time.

Then he did. "There's one last thing you need to know. I had a skull fracture that resulted in a traumatic aneurysm. No surgeon would come near it—as there's an almost hundred percent risk of crippling or killing me if they do—and no one can predict its fate. I can live with it and die of old age, or it can rupture and cost me my life at any moment."

Four

Maksim stared into Caliope's eyes and felt his marrow freeze. It was as if all life had been snuffed inside her.

He captured the hand frozen at his cheek. "I only told you so you'd know everything. But you don't need to be alarmed..."

She snatched her hand out of his hold, pushed out of his arms and heaved unsteadily to her feet, taking steps away, putting distance between them.

Without turning to face him, she talked, her voice an almost inaudible rasp. "You come seeking absolution and the sanctuary of a ready-made family, just because your crisis has changed your perspective and priorities. And you expect me to what? Agree to give you what you need?"

He opened his mouth, but her raised hand stopped his response, his thoughts.

She turned then, her voice as inanimate as her face. "Based on your own fears, you made the unilateral decision to cut me from you life without a word of explanation when I needed you most. And now you're back because you feel your life might end at any moment, and you want to grab at whatever you can while you can? How selfish can you be?"

When I needed you most.

That was what hit him hardest in all she'd said.

Had he been right just now, when he'd hoped she'd once felt more than desire?

He rose, approached her slowly, as if afraid she'd bolt away. "I never thought you needed me. You made it clear you didn't, only enjoyed me. It was one of the reasons I feared myself, since I started needing more from you than what you appeared to need from me. Had I known…"

"What would you have done? What would have changed? Would you have disregarded the 'overwhelming reasons' you had for leaving?"

He stabbed his hands in his hair. "I don't know. Maybe I would have told you what I just told you now and left it up to you to decide what to do. Maybe I would have stayed and taken any measures to ensure your safety."

"What measures could you have possibly taken against turning into the monster you feared you were bound to become?"

"I would have found a way. Probably some of the measures I intend to install now. Like telling Aristedes of my fears so he'll keep an eye on me. And having someone there all the time to intervene if I ever cross the line." He took her gently by the shoulders, expecting her to shake him off again. She didn't. She just stared up at him with those expressionless eyes that disturbed him more than any reaction from her so far. "I knew you had no use for the material things I offered, and I thought you didn't need anything else from me. Feeling of no use to you, then being unable to be with you, made me feel my existence was pointless. It wasn't conscious, but maybe I suggested that record-setting stunt to Mikhail wishing I'd self-destruct."

"Instead, you caused Mikhail's death. And ended up with a ticking time bomb in your head. A literal one, on top of the psychological one you feared would detonate at any time."

He hadn't expected cruelty. Not after she'd shown him such compassion. But her words were only cruel for being true.

His hands fell off her shoulders, hung at his sides. "Everything you say is right. But I am not after absolution, just redemption. I pledge I will do anything to achieve it, to earn your forgiveness, for the rest of my life."

"The life that can end at any moment."

Her bluntness mutilated him. Yet it was what he deserved. "As could any other's. The only difference between me and everyone else is that I'm aware of my danger, while others are oblivious to what's most likely to cause their death."

"But you're not only aware of a 'danger,' you're manifesting its symptoms quite clearly."

She must mean how much he'd deteriorated. He'd somehow thought this wouldn't be the point where she'd show no mercy.

"The aneurysm is a silent, symptomless danger. I'm far from back to normal because I didn't make any effort to get over the effects of my injuries and surgeries. But now I…"

"No."

The word hit him like a bullet. So harsh. So final.

But he couldn't let her end it without giving him a real chance. "Caliope…"

She cut him off again, harsher this time. "No, Maksim. I refuse your new deal."

"It's a proposal, Caliope."

She took a step back, then another, making him feel as if she were receding forever out of reach. "Whatever you want to call it, my answer is still no. And it's a final no. You had no right to think you can seek redemption at my expense."

"The redemption I'm seeking is *for* you. I'm offering you everything I can, what you just admitted you need."

"I only said you left at a time when I most needed you, not that I need you still. Which I don't. If you were thinking of me as you claim, the considerate thing to do was to stay away. The *last* thing Leo and I need is the introduction of your unstable influence in our lives. You had no right to force these revelations on me, to make those demands of me. And I'm now asking that you consider this meeting as having never happened, and continue staying away from me and Leo."

Every word fell on him like a lash, their pain accumulating until he was numb. But how could he have hoped for anything different?

In truth, he hadn't. He'd come here not daring to make any projections. Still, her coldness...shocked him. After baring his soul to her, he'd thought she'd at least let him down easy. Not for him, but because of who she was. He hadn't thought she had it in her to be so...ruthless. And for her to be so when he'd divulged his physical frailty—something beyond his control—was even more distressing.

It *had* been when he'd confided his medical prognosis that all the sympathy she'd been showing him had evaporated. And he had to know if his observations were correct. He hoped they weren't.

"Are you turning me down because you can't forgive me? Or because you don't want me anymore? Or...are you simply put off by my unstable physical condition?"

"I don't need to give you a reason for my refusal, just like you gave me none for your disappearance."

"I had to tell you the full truth, so you'd make an informed decision...."

"Thanks for that, and I have made such a decision. I expect you to abide by it."

He tried one last time. "If you're refusing because of my condition, I assure you it will never impact you or Leonid. If you let me be your husband and father for Leonid, you will never have anything to worry about in my life…or death."

"*Stop it*. I said no. I have nothing more to say to you."

He stared into those eyes. They smoldered with cold fire. Whatever compassion she'd shown him *had* been impersonal. Maybe only an expression of her anguish over Mikhail's loss, and she'd been sharing it with the one other person on earth who truly understood. Whatever she'd felt for him in the past he'd managed to kill, and in his current damaged state, everything he offered her now wasn't only deficient, but abhorrent to her.

And he couldn't blame her. It was his fault that he'd dared hope for what he'd never deserve.

He watched her turn stiffly on her heel, heading to the door. She was showing him out.

Following her, every step to that door felt as if it was taking him closer to the end. Depriving him of the will to go on. Like when he'd walked away from her before. But this felt even worse.

She held the door open, looking away from him as he passed her to step out of her domain, an outcast now.

He turned before she closed the door behind him, his palm a deterrent against her urgency to get rid of him.

Her gaze collided with his in something akin to…panic?

The next moment, what he'd thought he'd seen was gone, and she flayed him with stony displeasure at his delaying tactics.

But he had to ask one last thing.

"I'm not surprised at your rejection," he said, his voice

alien in his own ears, a despondent rasp. "I deserve nothing else. But will you at least, on any terms you see fit, let me see Leonid?"

Cali collapsed in bed like a demolished building.

She'd held it together until she'd closed the door behind Maksim, then she'd fallen apart. She'd barely reached the bathroom before she'd emptied her stomach.

But that hadn't purged her upheaval. A fit of retching, the likes of which she'd only suffered once before, had wrung her dry until she felt it would tear her insides up, until she'd almost passed out on the bathroom floor.

She'd dragged herself to the shower after the storm of anguish had depleted her, to dissolve in punishingly hot water what felt like even hotter tears.

She'd told Maksim no. A harsh, final no.

Now her every muscle twitched, her stomach still lurched.

The blows had been more than she could withstand. From the moment she'd found him standing on her doorstep to the moment he'd told her that he...he...

Her mind stalled again, to ward off that mutilating knowledge, swerved again to the lesser shocks. His unexpected return, the reason he'd left...then his proposal.

The first time he'd made it, her only reaction had been numb disbelief. It had been something she'd never visualized, not in her most extravagant fantasies of his return.

But by the time he'd told her everything and proposed again, her response had progressed from incredulity to delight. Acceptance wouldn't have been far behind.

Then he'd told her. Of his aneurysm. That he could be gone in a second. At any second.

And memories had detonated, with all the brutality of remembered devastation. Of what it had been like to love someone so much, to find out he had a death sentence hanging over his head then to lose him in unbearable abruptness.

Just the thought of repeating the ordeal had panic sinking its dark, bloody talons in her brain…and wrenching the life out of her.

Terror had manifested as fury. At him, for what he'd done to himself, and at fate, for taking Mikhail's life and blighting his with this sentence. And she'd lashed out at him.

Her harshness had only intensified at his disappointment.

Had he expected she'd be insane enough to say yes? Did he have no idea what it would do to her? Or how she felt at all?

She'd thought he'd felt her deepening emotions, and that had been why he'd left. But as it turned out, he'd been totally oblivious to her feelings, had just been focused on *his* needs and fears.

But she'd loved him when he'd been her noncommittal lover. How much more profoundly would she love him if he became her committed husband? She'd barely survived losing him to his seeming desertion. Losing him for real wouldn't be survivable.

Out of pure self-preservation, she'd told him no.

But she'd said yes to something else. To his seeing Leo.

She couldn't deny him his child. Especially now.

But now that she'd defused his need for redemption, without the influence of honor-bound obligation, he'd probably see Leo, awake this time, and realize that having a child in his life, even peripherally, was every bit as repugnant as he'd originally thought. Then it would just be a matter of time before he disappeared again.

This time she'd be thankful for his desertion.

Soon was all she could hope for. For no matter how brief his passage through her life would be this time, she had no hope it would be painless.

The next day, at 1:00 p.m., she'd just finished feeding Leo lunch when the bell rang. She almost jumped out of her skin and her heart stumbled into total arrhythmia.

Maksim. Arriving at the exact minute she'd asked him to. Though she'd been counting down the moments since he'd left last night, his actual arrival still jarred her.

She plucked Leo from his high chair, hooked him on her hip and smiled at him indulgently as he yammered in his usual gibberish, enthusiastically pointing out things all the way to the door.

Though she walked very slowly, feeling if she went any faster she'd fall flat on her face, Maksim didn't ring the bell again. She could imagine him, patiently waiting for her to answer the door. Maybe even expecting her not to. And with every step the temptation rose. To renege on her word, to ignore him until he went away for good.

But she couldn't do it. She only hoped he'd quench his curiosity, or whatever it was that made him want to see Leo. In a worst-case scenario, if he asked for a role in Leo's life, what he'd discarded before Leo was born, she'd be willing to negotiate. She really hoped he'd end up wishing not to be involved.

Drawing a breath, she smiled down at Leo once more, holding him tighter as if to prepare him for this meeting that she feared would change his life forever.

Then she opened the door.

Maksim towered across the threshold, his sheer physical presence and size overwhelming her as it always did. He looked as if he'd had as sleepless a night as hers, haggardness making him even more hard-hitting to her senses.

He was wearing light clothes for the first time ever, light beiges and cream, and it only made his gorgeousness overpowering.

She felt his agitation, but not because he was exhibiting it. He was containing it superbly, emanating equanimity, to observe Leo's acute response to moods. His eyes met hers briefly. Resignation at her rejection tinged their gold, along with the intensity that always made her every nerve burn. Then his eyes moved to Leo. And what came into them...

If she'd thought he'd looked moved when he'd beheld the sleeping Leo, now that he met his son's eyes for the first time, what stormed across his face, radiated from him was...indescribable. It was as if his whole being were focused on Leo, every fiber of him opening up to absorb his every nuance.

And Leo was looking back. As rapt, as riveted.

He wasn't used to other people, seeing even her family infrequently. With strangers, he usually buried his head in her bosom, watching them like a wary kitten from the security of her embrace. Leo had been his most uncertain around Aristedes, the most intimidating person he'd ever seen, until he'd gotten used to him. He should have reacted most unfavorably to Maksim, as he was even more daunting than Aristedes.

But it was just the opposite. His fascination with that huge, formidable, unknown being who was looking at him as if nothing but him existed in the world was absolute. It was the first time he'd reacted this openly, this fearlessly to anyone. It was as if he felt Maksim was different from everyone else. To him. She could almost *taste* their blood tie. It emanated from each of them, its influence instant and inextricable.

Suddenly, Maksim moved closer, intensity crackling from his eyes, making her instinctively press against the wall. When this squeezed a high-pitched gurgle from Leo, she rubbed her son's back soothingly and opened her mouth to tell Maksim not to test Leo's uncharacteristic acceptance.

Next second Leo squeaked again, but it was an unmistakable sound of delight this time. Then his six-toothed smile broke out.

Her nerves fired in surprised, agitated relief. But that was nothing to that smile's impact on Maksim. He looked as if a breath would blow him off his feet as he looked down at Leo's rosy-cheeked grin.

Then, as if touching priceless gossamer, he reached a hand that visibly shook to feather a caress down Leo's expectant face. Though he'd touched him before, it had been while Leo had been unaware. Now that same gesture, with Leo's sanction, became momentous. She watched it as it was given, received, felt as if a bond was being forged right before her eyes, felt caught in its cross fire, in the density of its weave, tangled in its midst.

"*Bozhe moy,* Caliope, how did I never notice how astounding children are? Or is it really because he's our son that I think him such a miracle?"

Her heart quivered at the ragged wonder in his voice, the agonized delight gripping his face. The hushed reverence in which he'd said "our son."

She had no words to answer his question, which wasn't one really, just this spontaneous venting of wonder she'd so many times longed to share with him. He was doing it with her now.

"Can I hold him?"

The rough, tentative whisper had tears squeezing out from her very essence.

It was as if he was asking for something so huge, he had little hope he was truly worthy of it. Yet he still braved asking, even as he looked as if he feared it was tantamount to asking her to relinquish a vital organ to him.

She shook her head as he turned his eyes to her. "It's not up to me. If he allows it, you can."

Maksim nodded as his reddened eyes tore from her face to Leo's, asking his baby for the privilege of his trust.

"Can I hold you, *moy malo* Leonid?"

My little Leonid. He talked to him as if he'd understand, at least the gentleness in his entreaty.

Next second, Maksim's sharp inhalation synchronized with hers. Leo held out his arms, hands opening and closing, demanding him to hurry and do what he'd asked for.

Maksim looked down on his hands, as if not sure what to do with them, before he swallowed audibly, raised his eyes to Leo and reached out to him.

A shudder shook through Maksim's great body as Leo pitched himself into his arms, as he received the little resilient body with such hesitancy and agitation.

A whimper escaped her. Leo hadn't hesitated, hadn't needed her encouragement before he threw himself at Maksim. Leo *had* recognized him. There was no other explanation.

Then she saw what snapped her control. Tears filling Maksim's wolf's eyes, accompanying a smile she'd never thought to see trembling on his lips, one of heartbreaking awe and tenderness. Her tears wouldn't be held back anymore.

They arrowed down her cheeks as she leaned against the wall so she wouldn't collapse, watching this meeting unfold between the two people who made up her world. Both father and son were so alike, so absorbed in their first exposure to each other, she felt her heart would shatter with the poignancy of it all.

Maksim held Leo with one arm, his other hand skimming in wonder over him. Leo allowed it all, busy exploring his father in utmost interest, groping his face, examining his hair and clothes. Maksim surrendered to his pawing, looking more moved with every touch than she had thought possible.

In the past, she'd never imagined this meeting would come to pass, so had never had any visualization of it. Even when she'd promised to let Maksim see Leo last night, she'd refused to anticipate his reaction, let alone Leo's. Any projection would have created dread or expectation, and she hadn't been able to deal with either. But this surpassed anything she could have come up with, couldn't be as transient as she'd hoped. It certainly wouldn't end here, at her door.

So she whispered, "Come in, Maksim."

Caliope had given Rosa, Leo's nanny, the day off in anticipation of Maksim's visit. Not that she'd thought he'd stay more than an hour or two. He'd again defied all her expectations.

In those two hours, he'd lost his inhibitions around Leo, made himself at home in her private domain and slotted effortlessly in her routine with her baby. The rest of the day flowed in a way she couldn't have dreamed of, in increasing ease and enjoyment.

There *were* many moments of tension throughout the day, seething with suppressed sensuality, but Leo's presence relieved those, his avid delight in Maksim drawing both of them back to the unit they formed around him.

Every now and then, Cali realized she was bating her breath. Expecting something to go wrong, to fracture the harmony that reigned over their company. But nothing did.

Maksim was at first uncertain what to do except let Leo do whatever he pleased with him. She soon had to warn him that he should firmly yet gently stop Leo if he went too far or demanded too much. Her son was still testing his boundaries, and he must be taught the lines he should never cross. Even with Maksim passing through their lives, she wouldn't have him upset the balance she'd gone to so much effort to establish, even if he didn't mean to.

Expecting Maksim to argue, he surprised her by bowing eagerly to her directive and doing everything to implement it.

She found herself looking at him so many times during the day, wondering how he could have ever feared himself. She couldn't imagine him being anything but that stable, indulgent, endlessly patient entity. Had his father ever possessed any of those qualities, and then lost them?

She couldn't believe that. Someone so volatile could never feign or experience such stability even for limited times. With every moment that passed, she became certain of one thing: whatever else he was, Maksim was not his father's son.

Leo on the other hand, was that and then some. She began to see even more similarities than those that had tormented her during the past year. Facial expressions, head tilts, glances, even grins— Now she saw actual ones from Maksim.

And Maksim was something else, too. An incredibly quick study. In doing anything for Leo, he obeyed her instructions to the letter and carried them out meticulously. Then came diaper-changing time.

He insisted on accompanying her for the unpleasant chore, stood aside watching her intently. A few hours later when that chore had to be repeated, he insisted on relieving her of it. Believing he'd balk at the…reality of Leo's diaper, she was again stunned as she watched that force of nature changing it without as much as a grimace of distaste, and with the earnestness and keenness that she'd seen him employ in negotiating multibillion-dollar business deals.

In between, he'd jumped into the fray to do everything for Leo. Even when she started doing something for Leo by force of habit, it was Leo who stopped her, demanded that his new adult slave do it instead.

She more than once began to tell Maksim to temper his enthusiasm, that he'd soon burn out at this rate. But every time she had to remind herself that it wouldn't hurt to let him indulge the novelty. Which wouldn't last long…

After feeding Leo the dinner she'd taught him how to prepare, he sat down on the ground with his son and let him crawl all over him, like a lion would let his cub.

Soon, Leo started to lose steam until he climbed on top of Maksim and promptly fell asleep on his chest.

Maksim lay there unmoving, unable to even turn his eyes toward her as she sat on the couch inches away from him.

Her lips twitching, even as her throat closed yet again, she took pity on him. "You can move. Nothing could wake him up now." When he didn't answer, she talked in an exaggeratedly loud whisper, "You *can* talk, you know?"

His whisper was barely audible. "Are you sure?"

"Certain. After six months of sleeping in fifteen-minute increments, until I thought I was destined for the insane asylum, he started sleeping like a log through the night."

He still whispered, "You mean I can rise and take him to bed and he still wouldn't wake up?"

"You can juggle him in the air and he wouldn't wake up."

It was still a while before he risked moving, and he still did it with the same caution he would employ defusing a bomb. It was so funny—especially since it seemed beyond him to do anything else—it had her dissolving in laughter.

He at last did rise, but still walked in slow motion all the way to Leo's cot, with her giggling in his wake.

But with the click of the door of Leo's room, she was dragged back to the terrible reality. That Maksim was here temporarily, that she had refused anything more with him for the best of reasons. And that she was on fire for him... and he clearly felt the same. She could feel his eyes boring into her back, his hunger no longer kept in check by Leo's presence.

And she had to deny them both.

He followed her in silence to the door, not even saying good-night as he exited her apartment.

She shook with relief and disappointment as she started to close the door, but he turned, his eyes the color of cognac as they brooded down at her.

"Can I have another day, Caliope?"

Her heart jumped with eagerness. But she couldn't heed it. She had to say no. It was the sane thing to do.

Today had come at a bigger price than she'd expected, the day's perfection the worst thing that could have happened to her. Another day together would definitely compound the damages.

But this man, who stood imploring her for another day with his child, had already lost so much—and continued to live with such pain and uncertainty. She'd always known Maksim could be trusted with her, and he'd proved that he could be trusted with Leo. She'd already told him a final no to anything between them. But Leo was his child, and he hadn't abandoned him as she'd believed.

Anyway, the perfection was bound to falter. Leo was a handful, was bound to wear him out. Maybe not in another day, but soon. And when Maksim pulled back to the position he'd originally wanted to occupy in his life, Leo would be too young to remember his transient closeness for long.

She'd be the one wrestling with need and dread. But how she felt wasn't reason enough to deny him his child, for as long as he needed to be close to him.

Fisting her aching hands against the need to reach out and drag him back in, she nodded in consent.

He still waited, needing a verbal affirmation.

Knowing she was going to pay for this in heartache but unable to do anything else, she whispered, "Yes."

Five

Cali had given Maksim the day he'd asked for.

But there had been one problem. He'd asked for another.

She'd granted him that, too, promising herself it would be the last. But she'd ended *that* day by agreeing, breathlessly, to let him be with them yet another day. Then another. And another.

Now it was ten weeks later. And Maksim had become a constant and all-encompassing presence in her and Leo's lives.

And with every passing minute she'd known she was causing them all irreparable damage by letting this continue. But she hadn't been able to put a stop to it, to go back to her status quo before Maksim's return.

She hadn't been happy, but she'd been coping well. But with Maksim sharing in Leo's day-to-day life with her, shouldering everything she allowed him to and offering more than she'd ever dreamed possible, she realized how much she'd been missing out on. She feared that his… completion was already indispensable.

She knew she'd always have the strength to go it alone if need be. But she no longer wanted to be alone, couldn't bear to think how it had felt when she had been, or to imagine how it would be again if she lost Maksim.

And she had to face it. She was insane. For letting him

invade and occupy her being and life again. And now that of Leo, who woke up every day expecting to see Maksim, and more often than not going to sleep in his arms. She kept placating herself that no matter how dependent on his presence Leo had become, he was far too young to be affected in any permanent way if Maksim was no longer there for any reason.

But where *she* was concerned, it was already too late.

Even if Maksim was gone tomorrow, she had dealt herself an indelible injury with these ten weeks in his company.

Though she hungered for him with a ferocity that had her in a state of perpetual arousal, without the delirium of their sexual involvement, she was levelheaded enough to appreciate so much more about him than ever before. She constantly discovered things about him that resonated with her mentally, commanded her respect for the man and human being, when previously she'd only had esteem for the businessman. He'd told her he was discovering those things about himself right along with her.

He, too, hadn't imagined he could possibly be with her without touching her, that he could be satisfied with just talking to her, discussing everything under the sun, agreeing on every major front. Even when they argued, it was stimulating and exhilarating, and he never tried to browbeat her into adopting his views or attempted to belittle hers. He listened more than he talked, seemed to like everything she had to say and admired all her choices and practices, whether in business or with Leo.

And she regularly found herself wishing he didn't, wishing he antagonized her or exasperated her in any way. How could she break free when he was being this all-around wonderful? She'd rather he started overstepping his limits and infringing on her comfort zones. It would be so much better if he became obnoxious or entitled. Or just anything that gave her reason to fear his existence in her life or to instigate a confrontation where she could cut him off.

But damn him… He didn't.

Worse still, it was no longer only her and Leo who'd been snared in his orbit. Her family and friends had entered the unsolvable equation, too.

Yeah, she'd told them. She'd had to. There'd been no hiding his presence in her life this time.

When pressed for details, she'd only said that they'd had an affair, he'd been involved in a serious accident and the moment he was back on his feet he'd come to see Leo.

Even with this dry account, their reactions to unmasking Maksim as Leo's father had been varied and extreme.

The women were stunned, delighted—not a little envious—and confused. They considered Maksim *the* catch of the millennium and couldn't imagine how she wasn't catching him, when he seemed to be shoving himself in her grasp.

The men thought she was plain bonkers that she wasn't already Mrs. Volkov, or at least putting the Volkov tag on Leo.

Selene, who had her own millennial catch and a similar history with him, thought it was only a matter of time before Maksim and Cali reached their own happy ending. It was Kassandra who had the most astute reading of the situation, convinced that there was so much more to the situation than her friend was letting on.

On the other end of the spectrum was Aristedes's reaction. After systematically interrogating her and finding out that Maksim had known about Leo from the start and had still left, nothing else had made an impression on him. Not that Maksim was back, or that he was offering her and Leo full access to his assets, name and time. That year she'd struggled alone had been unforgivable in his book. And no matter what Maksim was doing to rectify his desertion now, it would never wipe the slate clean. It was only after threatening to cut him out of her and Leo's lives that she was able to obtain a promise that Aristedes wouldn't act on his outrage.

"Did Maksim tell you he came to see me yesterday?"

The deep voice roused her from her reverie with a start. *Aristedes*. He was standing right before her.

She hadn't even noticed he'd walked into his expansive living room, where she'd come to take a call then stolen a few moments alone before dinner got underway. She replayed what he'd said and her heart clenched with dismay.

Maksim *hadn't* told her.

Throat suddenly parched, she could only shake her head in negation. What had Maksim done now?

Aristedes sat down beside her. "He wanted to 'chat' before we met for the first time in a family setting."

Aristedes and Selene were hosting one of their now-frequent family dinners, and her sister-in-law had insisted Cali invite Maksim. Cali had at first turned down the invitation. It was one thing for them to see him in passing with her. But to have a whole evening to investigate him up close?

When Selene wouldn't take no for an answer, Cali had been forced to tell her that Maksim would eventually exit her and Leo's life, and she preferred that he didn't become even more involved in it, making that departure even more difficult and unpleasant. Selene had only argued that if Cali indeed wanted Maksim's withdrawal, what better way to help her achieve that goal than by exposing him to her meddling Greek family? One evening of them en-

croaching on him would be the best way to convince him
to make a hasty exit.

Just because she'd known Selene would persist until
she got her way, Cali had grudgingly accepted. Not that
she had any hope whatsoever that Selene's scenario would
come to pass. From the evidence of the past ten weeks, she
was convinced Maksim would endure mad dogs shredding him apart to be with her and Leo. What was some
obnoxious intrusion compared to that?

Maybe she *should* sic Aristedes on him after all.

Though she doubted even the retribution of her almighty Greek brother would do the trick. Not only was
Maksim powerful enough to weather any damage Aristedes might inflict on him, she had a feeling he'd relish
submitting to his vengeance. He'd probably consider it a
tribute to her and to Leo, a penance for the time he hadn't
been there for them.

"Aren't you going to ask what he said?"

She glowered at Aristedes. "I'm sure you'll inflict the
details on me. Or else you wouldn't be sitting here beside
me. You do nothing arbitrarily."

"My opinion of you is confirmed with each passing
day." Though his tone was light, there was a world of emotion in his steel-hued eyes. Fury at the man they were discussing, protectiveness of her, amusement at her glibness
and shrewdness as he scanned her soul for the truth he
knew she was hiding. "You remain the most open-faced,
inscrutable entity I've ever known. When you want to hide
something, there's just no guessing it. I've known you had
a secret for over two years, but even when I investigated, I
came up empty-handed. How you hid something the size
of Maksim, I'll never know."

"You investigated me?"

At her incredulous indignation, his nod was wry and

unrepentant. "You think I'd leave my kid sister guarding a secret that implacably without worrying?"

"You mean without interfering." She scowled at him. "So what were your theories? That I was involved in some criminal activity or a victim to some terrible addiction?"

"Would that have been far from the truth? Weren't you involved with a dangerous scoundrel and, from the uncharacteristic behavior and length of your involvement, seriously addicted to him?"

Aristedes was one astute and blunt pain in the ass.

But she couldn't let one thing pass. "Maksim was never a dangerous scoundrel. As for my so-called uncharacteristic behavior with him, just ask any woman and she'd tell you that *not* being involved with him when I had the chance would have been incomprehensible, not the other way around."

Aristedes pursed his lips, clearly not relishing hearing her extol Maksim's attractions to women, starting with her.

"However irresistible you thought he was at the time, Maksim Volkov is certainly the last man I would have hoped you'd get involved with. He's not happily-ever-after material."

She snorted. "Isn't it fortunate then that I'm not, either?"

"And you still had a child with him."

"Something that I certainly didn't plan, and never considered pretext for a happy ending."

He lifted one formidable black brow. "So how do you define your situation right now? Where do you see this going?"

"Does it have to go anywhere? I would have expected you of all people to have the broadmindedness not to squeeze everything into the frame of reference of social mores. People can share a child without anything more between them."

"But that's not what Maksim thinks. Or wants."

God, what *had* Maksim told him?

Suddenly, it hit her. Aristedes, that gargantuan rat, was herding her with his elusive comments and taunts to goad her into asking what Maksim had said to him.

She skewered him with a glare that said she was onto him.

His storm-colored eyes sparked with that ruthless humor of someone who knew he always got his way.

"So…does your man like seafood?"

She blinked at the abrupt change in subject, at his calling Maksim "her man."

Then she slapped him on his heavily muscled arm. "I'm starting to think I liked you better when you were a humorless iceberg. Even when you developed a sense of humor, you wield it as a weapon."

"You mean he doesn't like seafood?"

The blatant mock-innocent pout earned him another whack.

He huffed a chuckle. "Just this time, I'll take pity on you, because I'm big that way…" She raised her hand threateningly, and he backed away, hands raised in mock defense. "…and because your deceptively delicate hand has the sting of a jellyfish." Her heart quivered as he paused. Then he exhaled dramatically. "*Nothing.* He told me a big, fat load of nada. You coached him well."

Her heartbeats frittered with the deflation of tension, with lingering uncertainty. Aristedes could be pulling her leg to make her spill info. She wouldn't put anything past him in his quest to get to the bottom of her situation with Maksim.

"He came offering his own version of what you told

us," he added. "Nothing more. He said he wouldn't make any excuses for leaving, that if I saw fit to punish him for it, he would 'submit'—*his words*—to any measures I exacted." He smiled sardonically, looking as if he relished the thought of taking Maksim up on his offer of a good, old-fashioned duel. "Then he went into great detail about how committed he was to Leo, and that if you agreed, he wanted to give him his name—but even if you didn't, the two of you have every right to all his assets, in life and death."

Her heart felt it had squeezed to the size of crumpled-up wrapper. "That's plenty more than what I told you."

Aristedes shrugged, looking annoyed, evidently disagreeing. "He didn't give me one drop of info on what happened between you in the past, no comment on what's going on in the present and zero projections for the future."

"What do you find so hard to line up in your head in an acceptable row? We had a…liaison, it resulted in a pregnancy then it ended. Now he's back because he wants to own up to his responsibilities toward his child, and he wants to be on good terms with the mother of his son."

Aristedes twisted his lips, his eyes wry. "He wants to be on the most intimate of terms with said mother. And don't even bother denying that. I'm a man who knows all the symptoms of wanting a woman so much it's a constant physical ache. I see my symptoms in him." He exhaled his displeasure with her. "Alas, I'm not as good a reader of women, and of you, I'm hopeless. That said, I still feel your answering attraction. So what's the problem? Is it your anti-marriage-or-long-term-commitment philosophy?"

She wanted to grab and kiss him for that way out. "Yes."

"Liar."

At his ready rebuttal, she shrugged. "You can think whatever you like, Aristedes. Bottom line is, I'm an adult, contrary to your inability to see me as one, and the way things stand between me and Maksim right now is the way I want them to be. When it's over…"

"Is this why you're so averse to letting him close?" he pounced, eyes crackling with danger. "You think he'll walk out on you again? Like our father? If he does that, I promise you, I'll skin him alive."

"Why, thanks for the lovely mental image, Aristedes. But no thanks. If he walks away, it's his right. Those were the terms of our liaison from the start. And then if he decides it's better for him not to be around us anymore, it certainly would be better for us not to have him around. So…give it a rest, will you? Let me conduct my life the way I see fit, and don't make me sorry I invited him here, or that I told you he's Leo's father in the first place."

"You didn't tell me. One glimpse of him all over you, with Leo all over him—his spitting image—outed you. It would have taken an imbecile not to put two and two together."

"You'll be one if you interfere, as I'll brain you."

"Any new reason you're threatening my husband with lobotomy?" Selene chuckled, striding toward them. "Just asking, since I happen to be very fond of his brain just the way it is."

Suddenly, terrible images cascaded in her mind's eye. Of Maksim, with his head cut open, surgeons exposing his brain…

"So what did he do now?"

Cali blinked as the overwhelming whoosh receded enough to let her hear the last snippet of Selene's question.

Exhaling her agitation, she grabbed the other woman's hand. "Your husband's doing the same thing you're doing. You both want to observe me and Maksim together—to judge the extent of our relationship and to try to influence its direction. And both of you will stop it right here, or I'll take Leo and leave and you can examine and probe Maksim on his own all you like. Then you won't see me again until you promise to behave."

Selene's other hand covered hers soothingly. "Hey, relax. We won't do a thing."

Selene turned gently warning eyes to Aristedes, asking his corroboration. As always, he immediately relented, this vast…adoration setting his steely gaze on tender fire. It was amazing to see this unstoppable force submitting, out of absolute love and trust, to his beloved's lead like this.

Maksim had been giving her the same reverent treatment.

And here he was now, entering the huge room, flooding it with his indomitable vibe and setting her perpetually racing heartbeat hammering. To compound his impact, he wasn't only laughing with his companions—her closest family and friends—he was holding Leo to his side, as if he was enfolding the heart that existed outside his body.

Seeing them together was, as always, the most exquisite form of torture.

Though Leo was his miniature replica, on closer inspection, she was in there, too. Maksim had pondered just yesterday that Leo made them look like each other. Her first reaction had been that this was preposterous, as they were as physically different as could be, but after catching a glimpse of all of them in a shop window, she'd had to admit he was right. Leo was the personification of everything they both were, as if the fates had mixed them up into a whole new being made of both. He did somehow make them look alike.

Maksim was preceded by his now-biggest fan, Leo's nanny. In the past ten weeks, Rosa had come to believe, right along with Leo, that the sun rose and set with Maksim and at his command.

When Cali had whimsically commented that Rosa had been struck by an acute case of hero worship, she'd looked at her disbelievingly and only said, "And you wonder why?"

Cali watched Maksim murmuring earnestly to Leo, as if agreeing on something confidential. She knew he was convincing their son to let Rosa take him, as he had something to do where no babies were allowed, then he'd be right back with him.

She didn't know who was more reluctant to leave the other: Leo, as he rubbed his eyes and grudgingly went into Rosa's arms, lips drooping petulantly, or Maksim, who looked as if he was relinquishing his heart to her. Rosa swept Leo away as all the nannies were taking the kids to Alex and Sofia's domain while the adult guests converged in the dining room.

Maksim turned and snared her in his focus across the distance. It was a good thing she was still sitting or his devouring smile would have knocked her down.

He prowled toward her like the magnificent golden-eyed wolf that he was, coming to escort her to dinner. She gave him a cold, clammy hand and rose shakily to her legs. He was glowing…for lack of another more accurate description. With vitality and virility.

In the past ten weeks he'd bounced back from his wraithlike state by the day, as if being with her and Leo had reignited his will to live, as if it infused him with limitless energy and was a direct line to a bottomless source of joie de vivre. He'd transformed back under her aching eyes to a state that even surpassed his previous beauty and vigor.

As he pulled the chair back for her at the table, she

could feel the combined scrutiny of everyone present on her, almost forcing her down under its weight.

As soon as they all settled into their respective seats, Selene beckoned to the caterer to start serving dinner. There was absolute silence as the first course was served, everyone's eyes busy studying both Cali and Maksim. Cali pretended to stir the creamy seafood soup, while acutely aware of Maksim as he sat beside her, taking everyone's examination in total serenity.

Praying that they'd all start eating or talking—or doing anything other than counting her and Maksim's breaths— she heaved a sigh of relief when Melina, sister number one, her second-oldest sibling after Aristedes, finally broke the silence.

"So Maksim…" Melina was looking at him in awe and perplexity, no doubt wondering how her little sister had such a man in her life at all, let alone have him willing to jump through hoops for her and his son. "You're a steel magnate."

Maksim put down his spoon respectfully, inclined his head at Melina. "I work in steel, yes."

"How's *that* for understatement?" That was Melina's husband, Christos. He was…crass, mostly with Melina, and that was what Cali called him, instead of Chris. "Volkov Iron and Steel Industries is among the world's top-five steel producers and is the leader in the Russian steel sector."

Maksim turned tranquil eyes to Christos. "Your information is up to date."

Christos looked very pleased with himself at Maksim's approval. "Yeah, I've been reading up on you. I'm very impressed with the dynamic growth you've achieved through the past decade that stemmed from continuing modernization of your production assets and adoption of state-of-the-art technology, not to mention integration into the global economy. And with the economic and marketplace difficulties in Russia, that's even more remarkable."

"And that means you're a multimillionaire, right?" That was Phaidra, sister number two.

Christos snorted. "Multi*billionaire,* Phai, like our Aristedes here. Maybe even a bigger one, too."

"You mean you don't know our exact net worth already, Christos, to decide who's…bigger?" Aristedes mocked.

Christos grinned at him, clearly still flabbergasted that he was in the presence of such men as his brother-in-law, and now his sister-in-law's "man," as Aristedes had called Maksim. "It's hard to tell when you two megatycoons keep exchanging your places on the list."

"But we're talking an obscene amount of money in either of your cases." That was Thea, sister number three, the youngest of her older sisters. "But all talk of mind-boggling wealth aside, are you going to give Leo your name?"

And Cali found her voice at last. "Oh, shut up, all of you. Can't you control your meddling Greek genes and try to keep your noses out of other people's business, at least to their faces?"

"You mean it's okay if we gossip about you behind your backs?" Thea grinned at her.

Cali rolled her eyes. "As long as I don't hear about it, knock yourselves out."

"If only you gave us straight answers," Phaidra said, "we wouldn't have to resort to any of this."

Melina nodded. "Yeah, do yourselves a favor and just surrender the info we want and you can go in peace."

Cali let her spoon clang into her bowl. "Okay, enough. I didn't invite Maksim here so you can dissect him and…"

"I don't mind."

His calm assertion aborted her tirade and had her mouth dropping open as she turned to him.

"What are you *doing?*" she whispered. "Don't encourage them or they'll have you for dinner instead."

"It's all right, Cali. Let them satisfy their…appetite. I'm used to this. Russian people aren't any less outspoken or passionate in their curiosity to find out the minute details of everyone around them, whether relatives or strangers. I feel quite at home."

"You mean they're as meddlesome and obnoxious? God, what kind of genes have we passed down to Leo?"

Aristedes cleared his throat, his baritone soaked in amusement. "Just letting you know that we can hear this failed attempt at a private aside. And that the soup is congealing."

Cali relinquished Maksim's maddeningly tranquil eyes and turned to her equally vexing brother. "Oh, shut up, Aristedes." Then, she rounded on the rest of them. "And all of you. Just eat. Or I swear…" She stopped, finding no suitable retribution to threaten them with.

"Or what, Cali?" Thea wiggled her eyebrows at her. "You're going to pull one of your stunts?"

Phaidra turned to Maksim. "Did she ever tell you what she used to do when she was a child when we didn't give in to her demands as the spoiled baby of the family?"

Maksim sat forward, all earnest attention. "No. Tell me."

From then on, as her siblings competed to tell Maksim the most "hilarious," aka *mortifying,* anecdote about her early years, the conversation became progressively livelier. Maksim was soon drawing guffaws of his own with his dry-as-tinder wit, until everyone was talking over each other and laughing rambunctiously. Even Aristedes got caught up in the unexpectedly unbridled gaiety of the gathering. Even she did.

It was past 1:00 a.m. when everyone got up to leave, hugging Maksim as if he were a new brother. Then Cali waited with Aristedes and Selene as Maksim went to fetch Rosa and Leo. He came back carrying everything, to Rosa's continued objections, with a sleepy Leo curled contentedly in his embrace.

As thanks and goodbyes were exchanged, she watched the two towering male forces shake hands and almost laughed, sobbed and stomped her foot all at the same time.

Aristedes's glance promised Maksim that live skinning if he didn't walk the straight and narrow, and Maksim's answering nod pledged he'd submit to whatever Aristedes would inflict if for any reason he didn't. The pact they silently made was so blatant to her senses, as it must be to Selene's, that it was at once funny, moving and infuriating.

She barely held back from knocking their magnificent, self-important, terminally chivalrous heads together.

They left, and after dropping Rosa off, Maksim drove back to Cali's apartment. In her building's garage, he enacted the ritual of taking her and Leo up, shouldering all the heavy lifting, and accompanying her to put Leo in his crib. Then without attempting to prolong his stay, he walked back to the door.

Before he opened it, he turned to her, his eyes molten gold in the subdued lighting. "Thank you for this evening with your family, Caliope. I really enjoyed their company."

She could only nod. Against all expectations, she'd truly enjoyed the whole thing, too. And it just added another layer of dismay and foreboding to their situation.

"They all love you very much."

She loved them, too, couldn't imagine life without them. She sighed. "They're just interfering pains with it."

"It's a blessing to have siblings who have your best interests at heart, even if you have to put up with what you perceive as infringements." Maksim sighed deeply. "I always wished I had siblings."

Her heart contracted so hard around the jagged rock she felt forever embedded inside it.

Did he mean what...?

Before the thought became complete, forming yet another heartache to live with, he swept her bangs away, his gaze searing her as it roamed her face.

She thought he'd pull her into his arms and relieve her from her struggle, end her torment, give her what she was aching for.

He didn't. He only looked at her with eyes that told her how much craving he was holding back. And that he wouldn't act on it, except with her explicit invitation.

Then he said, "Will you come to Russia with me, Caliope?"

Six

Maksim saw the shock of his request ripple across Caliope's face. This had come out of the blue for her.

It had for him, too.

He could feel an equally spontaneous rejection building inside her, but he couldn't let her vocalize it.

Her lips were already moving when he preempted her. "My mother lives there. It would mean the world to her if she could see her grandson."

At the mention of his mother, the refusal she'd undoubtedly been about to utter seemed to stick in her throat.

She swallowed, the perfection of her honeyed skin staining with a hectic peach. "But…Russia!" He waited until the idea sank in a bit further. Then she added, "And you're proposing…we go right away?"

Relieved that he'd stopped her outright refusal in its tracks and that they were already into the zone of negotiation, he pressed his advantage. "It would be fantastic for her to attend her grandson's first birthday."

It took a moment before the significance and timing of that milestone hit her with their implications.

And she exclaimed, "But that's two weeks away."

"A trip to Russia shouldn't be for less than that."

"But if it's for Leo's birthday, we can leave a day or two beforehand."

He bunched his hands into fists, or he would have reached for her, crushed her against him, kissed her senseless until she said yes to anything he asked.

He held back, as he now lived to do. "I know she would appreciate as much time with Leo as possible, and I'm sure she'd love to prepare his birthday celebration and host it in her home."

That made her eyes widen. "Her home? Not yours, too?"

"I don't live with her, no."

That seemed to derail her meandering train of thought, bringing that gentle, curious contemplation he was getting used to to the forefront. "Then where *do* you live? I never got around to asking. When you're not traveling on business and staying in hotels?"

"If you're asking if I have a home, the answer is no."

He almost added he'd only ever wished for a home with her. The only home he wanted now was with her and Leo.

He didn't. She'd already told him she wouldn't be his home. And she had every right to refuse to be. Her first and last duty was to protect herself and Leo from his potential for instability and premature expiration. He should be thankful—he *was* thankful she was allowing him that much with her, and with Leo. He shouldn't be asking for more.

Not that what he should feel and what he *did* feel held any resemblance. He went around pretending tranquility and sanity when he was going insane with wanting more.

Considering his answer about having no home a subject ender, she resumed her unease about the original one. "This is…so sudden, Maksim…and I'm not prepared. I have work…."

"Most of your work is on the computer, and you can work anywhere. And I'll make sure you regularly have the peace and quiet you need to."

"But Leo…"

"He'll be with me while you work, and with my mother. And she has a *lot* of help. And we'll take Rosa, too."

The peach heat across her sculpted cheekbones deepened. "Seems you have this all figured out."

It was all coming to him on the fly. But it didn't make it any less ferocious, the need that was now hammering at him to whisk her away, to rush her and Leo to his mother's side, to connect them before he…

Exhaling the morbid and futile thought, he shrugged, hoping to look calm and flexible about the whole thing, so he wouldn't scare her off. "Not really. I only thought of it right now."

Her gaze became skeptical. "You mean you didn't plan to eventually take Leo to see his grandmother before?"

The strangest thing was that he hadn't. Now, as she confronted him with the question, the truth suddenly dawned on him. "No, I didn't. I no longer plan anything ahead."

Her pupils expanded, plunging her incandescent heaven-hued eyes into darkness. No doubt remembering why he didn't.

He hadn't brought up his condition since he'd admitted it to her. But as Caliope's and Leonid's closeness infused him with boundless energy and supercharged his life force, he'd almost forgotten all about it. He felt so invincible now that most times he couldn't believe there was anything wrong with him. But he *had* been told it was a silent danger.

Now her unspoken turmoil was more unbearable than sensing that ticking time bomb she'd said he had inside his head. He had to take her thoughts away from this darkness.

The only way he knew how was to give her back the control that his condition, something so out of anyone's control, deprived her of. "Or I still make plans, but only in work. With you and Leo I can't, since it's not up to me to make any plans."

As he'd hoped, the terrible gloom that had dimmed her vibe lifted, as her thoughts steered away from the futility.

She lowered her eyes while she considered her verdict, and that fan of lashes eclipsed her gaze and hid her thoughts. His lips tingled, needing to press to their silken thickness, closing those luminous eyes before melting down those sculpted cheeks, that elegant nose, to her petal-soft lips. Just looking at those lips made his go numb with aching to crush them beneath his, with clamoring to tangle his tongue with hers, to drain her taste, to fill her needs. For he could feel them, and they were as fierce as his. But he knew she wouldn't succumb to them. The price was too high for her, when she had Leo to think about.

He understood that, accepted it. He could barely function with suffering it, but he'd known that if he pushed through the boundaries she needed to maintain, she'd slam the door in his face. And he would put up with anything to have whatever she would allow him of herself, of Leonid.

But now that the idea had taken root, it was no longer about him. It was about his mother. And he decided to use this as a point of persuasion, since it was true.

A finger below Caliope's chin brought her now-turbid gaze up to his. "I didn't feel I had the right to ask this before, when I thought my admission into your lives would be short-lived. I couldn't risk letting my mother know of Leonid only to lose him again when I lost my unofficial visitation rights. If you feel you're not going to end those, or that even if you do you wouldn't cut my mother off from Leonid's life by association, let me take you to meet her."

"Maksim...don't..."

At her wavering objection, he pressed on with his best argument. "I always thought nothing could possibly make up for what she'd lost and suffered. But if there's one thing that can heal her and make it all up to her, it's Leonid."

She hadn't been able to say no.

How could she have when Maksim had invoked his mother?

She actually felt ashamed he'd had to, that she hadn't been the one to consider the woman and her right to know Leo, her only grandson. She'd known Tatjana Volkova was alive, but she'd shied away from knowing anything more about her. What Maksim had told her of his mother had been so traumatic she'd avoided thinking of her so she wouldn't have to dwell on what the woman had gone through. It had to have been so much worse than what her own mother had suffered, though *that* much less abusive experience had undeniably altered her own attitude toward life and intimacy. She had too much to deal with what with her situation with Maksim, and she couldn't add to her turmoil by introducing more of Tatjana's sufferings into her psyche.

But not only was Leo Tatjana's only grandchild, she was the only grandparent he had. He had a right to know her, just as Tatjana had more right to him as his grandmother than any of Cali's own family.

There had been no saying no to Maksim in this. Nor could she have played for more time. The timing was very significant. A first birthday was a milestone she couldn't let his mother miss. And she'd also bought his argument of going there ahead of time and letting Leo's grandmother share the joy of preparing that event.

This meant that she didn't have time to breathe as she threw together a couple of suitcases for the two weeks Maksim had said they'd stay. And the very next morning, she found herself, along with Leo and Rosa, being swept halfway across the world, heading to a place she'd never been or ever thought she'd be: Maksim's motherland.

The flight on his private jet had been an unprecedented experience. She was used to high-end luxuries, from her own financial success, and Aristedes's in-a-class-of-its-own wealth. But it was Maksim's pampering that went beyond anything she could have imagined. She squirmed at how much care he kept bestowing on them. Though he remained firm when needed with Leo, seamlessly keeping him in check with the perfect blend of loving indulgence and uncompromising discipline.

So she couldn't use spoiling Leo as a reason to demand he dial down his coddling, and he insisted that since she and Rosa were responsible adults, his efforts wouldn't spoil *them* and they should just sit back and enjoy it.

She couldn't speak for Rosa, but he was definitely wrong in her case. He was spoiling her beyond retrieval, taking her beyond the point where being without him would be impossible.

And self-destructive fool that she was, she'd only put up a token resistance, as halfhearted as all those other instances over the past ten weeks, before finally surrendering to his cosseting and reveling in his attention and nearness.

And now here she was. In Russia.

They'd landed in a private airport an hour ago. They were now in the limo that had been awaiting them at the jet's stairs, heading toward his mother's home. Rosa and Leo were in the limo's second row, while she and Maksim sat in the back.

And to top it all off? The city in Northern European Russia that they were now driving through was called Arkhangel'sk. *Archangel.*

How appropriate was that? For it to be the hometown

of the archangel who was sitting beside her and acting the perfect guide?

"The city lies on the sides of the Dvina River near its exit into the White Sea…" he pointed at the river they were driving along "…and spreads for over twenty-five miles along its banks and in its delta's islands. When Peter the Great ordered the creation of a state shipyard here, it became the chief seaport of medieval Russia. But in the early eighteenth century, the tsar decreed that all international marine trade be shifted to St. Petersburg, leading to the deterioration of Arkhangel'sk. The decree was cancelled forty years later, but the damage was done and Baltic trade became more relied on."

Her gaze swept the expansive stone sidewalk running by the river, trying to imagine how the city had looked all those centuries ago when Russia was an empire. She had a feeling it hadn't changed much. It had an authentic old-world vibe to it, echoes of long enduring history in every tree and stone and brick forming the scene.

"So did Arkhangel'sk's economy revive at all before *you* put it back on the map?"

Clearly gratified with her interest on his account, he nodded. "It did somewhat, at the end of the nineteenth century when a railway to Moscow was completed and timber became a major export. And until fifteen years ago, the city was primarily a center for the timber and fishing industries."

Her gaze melted down his face as she marveled yet again at his beauty, at the power and nobility stamped on his every feature. "Until you came along and turned it into the base for Russia's largest iron and steel works."

His lips twisted. "That implies that I switched its historical focus from timber and fishing to steel, when I only added that industry to the existing ones."

"And revived and advanced the other two beyond recognition." His dismissive shrug was another example of how he never took any opening to blow his own horn. She persisted. "I've been reading up on your contributions here. People no longer say this city is named after the archangel Michael, who'd been designated as the city's protector centuries ago, but after your nickname here as its current and far more effective benefactor."

His eyes glowed. Not with pride at his gargantuan accomplishments, which he treated with a pragmatic, almost indifferent matter-of-factness. His gratification seemed to be on account of her investigating said accomplishments and finding them—and him—worthy of admiration. It seemed to be her own opinion that counted to him, far more than what he believed of his actual worth.

This explicit reaction, whenever she lauded his actions or complimented his character in any way, always left her with a knot in her throat and a spasm in her heart.

To realize he needed her validation was at once delightful and heartbreaking. She'd lost so many opportunities to show him her appreciation during their year together, when she'd been so busy hiding the extent of her emotional involvement that she hadn't given him his due in fear he'd suspect it and it would change everything. Now that she had stopped pretending that she didn't see his merits and freely expressed her esteem, they were in this impossible situation....

She turned her eyes to the scenery rushing by her window, of that resplendent subarctic city draped in a thin layer of early November's pristine snow, and saw almost none of it as she wrestled with another surge of regret and heartache.

After an interval of silence, Maksim resumed his narration, continuing to captivate her with anecdotes of the city and region.

Then they turned onto a one-way road flanked by trees, their dense, bare branches entwining overhead in a canopy.

"We're here."

Her heart kicked into a higher gallop at his deep announcement.

This was really happening. She was going to meet Maksim's mother, and spiral further into the depths of his domain.

Swallowing the spike of agitation, she peered out of the window as they passed through thirty-foot-high, wrought-iron gates adorned with golden accents into a lushly land-scaped park. She'd been to stunning palaces that had parks of this magnitude before, but those had been tourist attractions. She'd never seen anything like this that was privately owned.

The park seemed endless, nature weaved into the most delicate tapestry. Cut-stone passages wound through par-terres of flowers and trimmed hedges, meeting at right or diagonal angles, with marble statues situated at each inter-section, and lined with myrtle trees formed into spheres or cones and huge mosaic vases before converging on a circular pavilion.

"This is the French 'stage' of the park," Maksim said. "Then in the late eighteenth century, the Russian nobil-ity's taste changed, explaining the zone we'll pass through next."

As soon as the limo left the pavilion behind, Cali saw what Maksim meant. There was a dramatic change in the park to something even more to her liking than the perfect geometry she'd just seen. An English landscape garden, an idealized version of nature, with winding paths, tun-nels of greenery, picturesque groves of trees, lawns and pavilions, all with that dusting of snow, turning it into a winter wonderland.

She turned her eyes to him, awed. "This place is… breathtaking. Did you buy it for your mother when you started your steel business here?"

"No, this is where I grew up."

Her mouth dropped open at that revelation. "This is your family estate?"

That tight shrug again, which she by now knew indicated a subject he was loath to discuss. "It's a long story." His tone suddenly gentled. "The estate is called *Skazka,* by the way."

She repeated the word slowly. "*Skazka.* Fairy tale. How appropriate. This does look like the setting of one."

"Maybe a horror tale. At least in the past." A shadow crossed his face as he referred to the time when his father had been alive. "Now it's just the place my mother considers home." His eyes brightened. "But you never told me you knew any Russian. *Skazka* isn't a common word, which can only mean you know more than the basics."

She'd kept it to herself so far, had just savored understanding his spontaneous exclamations and endearments.

Feeling it was time to come clean, she attempted a grin. "I started learning it when we first…" she cleared her throat awkwardly "…started seeing each other."

His gaze lengthened, heated, as if he was seeing a new facet to her and it sent his appetites flaring.

She expected him to try to draw a confession that she had learned Russian for him. But, as always, she couldn't predict him.

One finger feathered her cheek in a trail of fire, his eyes also burning as they mimicked its action. "So you understood everything I've been saying to you." She nodded, and an enigmatic expression entered his eyes. Then he broke contact and gestured straight ahead. "And here's the mansion."

She tore her gaze to the place that had been the setting for the life-altering ordeal that had put him on a path of self-destruction, causing that chain reaction that might *still* succeed in detonating their lives.

The massive building was imposing, majestic. Built in the architecture of a summer country house in the neo-classical style with Grecian influences, it was so huge she thought it must house dozens of rooms. Plastered planks painted in soft beiges and cream comprised the exterior facade. The columned portico had a wide ramp leading to the front door, for cars now, but it must have been for carriages with horses back in the time it had been built. She could almost see a scene from that era as a carriage arrived, with servants rushing out the front doors to hold the horses while guests descended.

As soon as the limo stopped at the front door, Maksim stepped out, and she waited as she'd learned to for him to come around and open her door for her. He covered the fast-asleep Leo securely, then carried him out in his car seat.

In a few minutes, they were walking from the biting cold into the mansion, where it was perfectly warm. Drinking in her surroundings, Cali stared up into a vestibule with a thirty-foot ceiling with walls painted to resemble marble and columns to reflect the porticos.

Without stopping, Maksim led them to a reception room with an ornate fireplace and an oven decorated in colored tiles, with the rest of the decor and furnishings displaying the artistic traditions in Russia at the time the mansion had been built. Everything looked as if had been just finished, which could only mean Maksim had had this place restored to its original condition.

And she again wondered how and why he had, when this place held nothing but horrific memories.

She shook away the speculations as Maksim led them in silence to another reception room, decorated with tapestries depicting the scenes from the parks. Between the tapestries, tall windows looked out onto the lake and gardens. And at one of those windows, with her back to them, clearly unaware of their silent entry, there she stood.

Maksim's mother.

The woman in her late sixties was very tall, which meant she'd been even taller as a young woman, much taller than Cali. This must be where Maksim had inherited his prodigious height. Or maybe he had from both parents. Tatjana Volkova looked like a duchess from the time of the tsars, with her thick dark hair held up in a sleek, deceptively simple chignon, and her statuesque figure swathed in a flowing, cream-colored pantsuit, with exquisite lace accents at the collar and cuffs.

"Mamochka."

Cali jumped at the word, the most loving form of mother in Russian, murmured with such fathomless tenderness in Maksim's magnificent voice.

It had the same effect on his mother, who suddenly lurched and swung around at the same time and stood facing them for a moment of paralysis that echoed Cali's. Then she exploded in motion.

Cali stood beside Maksim, unable to breathe as the woman streaked toward them, marveling at the fact that she was looking at the older, female version of Maksim.

Then she was in her arms, being hugged with the fervor of a mother who at last had her long-lost daughter in her arms.

Cali surrendered to the older woman's need to express her emotions physically. She felt her hugs were fueled by a long-held belief she'd never have more than Maksim in the world, and Cali was the reason she now had more— a grandson.

When Tatjana finally withdrew, she still held her by the shoulders, her hazel eyes, a slightly darker hue of Maksim's, shining with tears. "Caliope, my dear, thank you so much for coming to see me. I can't tell you how much I appreciate it. I'm so sorry to drag you all the way here. I wanted to fly to you as soon as Maksim told me of you and Leonid, but my son insisted you'd be the ones who came to me."

"You fear flying, *Mamochka,*" Maksim said. "And there was no reason to put you through that, even in my company."

Cali nodded. "You mustn't do anything you're uncomfortable doing. Leo can handle flying, and it's my pleasure to come to you."

Tatjana only grabbed her and kissed her again, and her eyes filled more as she drew away. Then she transferred her gaze to Maksim, or more specifically, to what he was carrying: Leo.

"*Bozhe moy,* Maksim… *On vam, kogda vy byli yego vozrasta.*"

My God, Maksim… He is you, when you were his age.

Cali's swallowed that ball of thorns lodged in her throat, tears sprouting in her eyes. The anguished joy that gripped Tatjana's face was shearing in intensity, just like Maksim's had been, hitting her again with the power of that same instant connection to Leo.

She knew Leo had people who loved him, all her family. But Maksim and Tatjana were the only two who would love him more than life itself, just like she did.

She touched Tatjana, running a soothing hand down

her slim arm, her voice not as steady as she hoped. "Wake him up."

"I can't…. He looks so peaceful…like an angel."

Cali's lips trembled on a smile. "And he'll be a devil if he sleeps any more. He's been asleep most of the trip and in the car, and if he doesn't wake up now, he won't sleep tonight. And between you and me, I'd really rather not have his rhythm thrown out of whack. So go ahead, wake him up."

Tatjana's wiped away her tears. "Will you do it? I don't want him to get startled, finding a stranger rousing him."

Cali decided to heed Tatjana's worry. She wanted this first meeting to go perfectly, so why risk initial discomfort?

But she had a better idea, something Tatjana would appreciate seeing far more: Maksim waking his son up.

She looked at Maksim, her request explicit in her eyes. The flare of thankfulness in his almost blinded her.

Then he put the chair on the ground, crouched to his haunches beside Leo, kissed his forehead and cheeks, then crooned to him in the most loving, soul-stirring voice, "*Prosypat'sya, moy lyubimaya...* Wake up, my beloved Leonid."

Tears burned at the magnitude of love that poured from Maksim. She knew Leo basked in it, awake and asleep, thrived with it more daily, becoming progressively happier…stronger. She also loved how Maksim always talked to him in both English and Russian, making sure Leo would grow up speaking both fluently. He also urged her to speak in Greek to Leo, so their son would be raised with every facet of his heritage. Though Greek didn't come naturally to her, since she'd lived only six years on Crete before Aristedes took them to America, she did what he asked. And Leo was already trying out words in all three languages.

Leo stirred, stretched noisily as he blinked up sleepily at his father. Maksim's heart was in his smile as he gently caressed his son's downy head, delight radiating out of him as Leo reached out and clung around his neck, burying his face into his chest.

She heard a sharp sob, thought it was her own. It never ceased to overwhelm her, the depth of the bond both man and son had developed in the past weeks.

But it was Tatjana who was now crying uncontrollably. Anxiety crept up Cali's spine that Leo would see his grandmother for the first time like this, and might react to Tatjana's tears like he had to hers when she'd once let him see them.

But Maksim didn't seem worried as he scooped up an immediately alert Leo and approached his mother, talking to him in this soft, confidential way he reserved only for him. "I want you to meet someone who loves you as much as I do."

She could swear Leo understood, even nodded his consent; then he transferred his attention to the weeping woman.

Cali bated her breath, her nerves tightening in expectation of Leo's reaction. For long moments as Maksim brought him within arm's length of Tatjana, Leo just gazed at her as her sobs increased and her tears poured thicker, his watchful eyes gleaming with curiosity, his rosebud mouth a wondrous O.

Then she whispered, *"Ya mogu derzhat' vas, moy dragotsennyye serdtsa?"*

Can I hold you, my precious heart?

Leo looked at her extended arms, a considering look coming over his face. Then he swung his gaze to Maksim, then back to Tatjana, as if noticing the resemblance and realizing who Tatjana was. Then his smile broke out.

Next moment, he pitched himself from Maksim's arms and into Tatjana's. With a loud gasp, the older woman received him in trembling arms, hugging him fiercely, her sobs shaking him and her whole frame. But Leo only squealed in delight and hugged her back.

He'd apparently recognized that her tears weren't ones of misery but of joy, and reacted accordingly, with the pleasure of being the center of attention and the pride of being the source of such overpowering emotions.

Cali found her tears flowing freely, too, then found herself where she yearned to be every second of every day… in Maksim's arms, ensconced against his heart.

She looked up at him, to catch his reaction, and found him looking down at her, his eyes full.

He held her tighter to his side. "*Spasiba, moya dorogoya.* Thank you, for Leo…for everything."

Her tears poured faster as she sank into his embrace, having no words to express her own gratitude—for him, for this, the family she and Leo suddenly had. And mingling with all that joy was the dread that this would only be temporary. His eyes told her no words were needed, that he understood her upheaval. Then hugging her more securely, he turned his loving gaze to his mother and child, clearly savoring those poignant moments.

She leaned against his formidable shoulder and wondered how this would end.

And when it did end, since nothing this good could possibly last, would she survive it?

Seven

Maksim sighed as he gazed out his bedroom window.

Not that it was really his, just the suite he occupied when he stayed here. The one he'd had as a child he'd turned into part of a living area his mother used for her weekly gatherings with her various public-work committees. His mother had given Caliope and Leonid the suite across from him.

He'd almost moved out when she had.

Being in constant proximity to Caliope during the day was something he could relish…and withstand. During the nights, to feel her so close, to visualize her going about her nightly routines was sheer torture.

That first night, he'd lain in bed imagining he could hear her showering, feel the steam rising to shroud her lush body, the lather sliding tantalizingly over her every swell and into her every dip, the water sluicing over her curves, washing suds away. Then he'd seen her drying her hair until it cascaded around her smooth shoulders in a glossy mass, applying lotion to her velvet flesh, slipping into a silky nightgown, sinking into bed between the covers with a sigh of pleasure. All those things he'd so many times done for her as she'd surrendered to his ministrations, as he'd pampered her, indulged her, possessed her all through that magical year. Exquisite pleasures he'd never have the privilege of having again.

He'd woken up aching, wrecked, intending to hole up somewhere on the far side of the mansion. But she'd exited her bedroom suite at that same moment, a smile of pure joy flashing at the sight of him, and he'd known. He'd put up with any level of frustration and agony for the possibility of a moment like this.

The last time he'd stayed here had been six months ago, when he'd finally succumbed to his mother's fretting and had come visiting her. He'd tried everything to put off that visit, hating to let her see him in his condition back then.

She'd been horrified when she'd laid eyes on him, but she'd thought he was just desolate over Mikhail's death. He'd let her think that. It had given her hope he'd eventually climb out of the abyss of despair and regain his health. He hadn't even thought of telling her the truth.

Then a miracle had happened. He'd reached out to Caliope, and though she'd refused to let him back into her own life, to bestow her intimacy on him again, she'd let him into her precious family unit with Leo. Beyond all expectations, she had given him a closeness he'd never thought possible to have with her, or with anyone else after Mikhail.

She'd become his friend, his ally, when before she'd only been his lover. Every minute with her made him realize how much he'd been missing—with her, in life. He couldn't help but keep envisioning how much deeper it could all be if she let him cross that final barrier into passion once more.

But he would never ask for it. What she continued to give him was enough, more than enough. The past ten weeks had been a heaven he'd never dared dream existed, or that he would ever be worthy of having anyway. He still couldn't believe it was really happening.

But it was. He was beholding it in the gardens his suite overlooked. They were talking, laughing and reveling in being together. Caliope. Leonid. And his mother. Everything that made his heart beat, that formed his world and shaped his being.

For the past two weeks, he'd often found himself overwhelmed with so much emotion, so much gratitude, he had to force himself to breathe. Both Leonid and Caliope had taken to his mother as he could have only hoped they would. Leonid's instant attachment had been the far less surprising one. That sensitive, brilliant baby had recognized his mother for what she was to him, and as an extension of the father he had accepted and claimed from the very first instant. But it was Caliope's delight in his mother that sometimes threatened to crush his heart under its significance.

During one of their intimate fireside chats, she'd confided that she'd never really had a mother. Her own had been a shadow by the time Caliope was born, and had died when she'd been not yet six. Now it felt to Maksim as if in his own mother she'd found that maternal presence and influence she'd never known she'd missed, let alone craved. While it also felt his mother had found the daughter she'd lost in Caliope.

To crown the perfection, tomorrow was Leonid's first birthday. He'd had only the last three months of that first precious year, and he ached for every minute he'd wasted, lost, not been there for Caliope and his son. But he would be there for them both from now on. Till his dying day.

Although he lived every second with them as if it would be his last, he prayed that day wouldn't come anytime soon. Nevertheless, he'd put everything in order for all of them, just in case. And now that he had the peace of mind that Cali and Leo's future was secure, he could focus on making plans as if he'd live forever. He now had every reason to hope he would live as long as humanly possible. He'd never felt more alive or robust. His energy levels were skyrocketing, and he continued to grow more vigorous with each passing day, as if his will to live had come into existence. Before Caliope and Leonid, he'd only had a will to survive, to decimate obstacles and reach the next level, then the next. But all that hadn't amounted to living. Not without them filling his heart and making it all worthwhile.

He sighed again at the sight of them, let it permeate his soul with its sheer beauty and magic.

How he loved them all.

He didn't know how long he remained standing there, hoarding yet more priceless memories, before he roused himself. He had plans for today and he'd better get going so he'd have time to see them all through.

He rushed down to the gardens, and as he approached the trio, they turned to him, eager to see him. And he wondered again how he could possibly deserve all that.

But if he never had before, he would now. And he'd revel in every single second of their blessings and give them back a thousandfold, until he'd given them all that he was.

His gaze went first to his mother. In spite of all the ordeals she'd suffered, she'd always remained strong, stable, even, most of the time, amazingly sunny. But now… Now she radiated *joy*. And it was all thanks to Leonid. And Caliope.

His gaze moved next to Leonid. That little miracle that always had his insides melting with a million emotions, half of them sublime and the other half distraught. He wondered again how parents survived loving their children and worrying about them this much. But he was learning how, with Caliope's constant support and guidance. This again led him to wonder how his father had been able to hurt him. He'd rather have his arms hacked off before he even upset Leonid.

Yes, he was now certain. He had none of his father's sickness. And not because his ordeal had reconfigured him. He just didn't have it in him. All his dread now was from external sources. Life had so many dangers, it suffocated him at times to think of Leonid being exposed to any of them.

But even with the constant fears that had become part of his consciousness, he wouldn't change a thing. He wanted nothing but to be Leonid's father, to give him the safest, happiest, most adjusted and accomplished life.

He'd left looking at the center of his universe, the spark of his existence, for last. For she was where his gaze would stay, where his heart would lie down to rest. Caliope.

How was it possible that she was more beautiful every time he beheld her?

Her radiant smile rivaled that of the bright Russian autumn sun. Her naturally sun-kissed complexion glowed with vitality in the cold, her caramel-gold hair gleamed and undulated in the tranquil breeze and her azure eyes were incandescent with warmth and welcome. Her lips, flushed and dewy, spread to reveal those exquisitely uneven white teeth in that smile that splintered his heart with its beauty. He hardened all over, as he always did when he even thought of her, which was almost constantly. Now, with her so close in the flesh, warding off the blow of longing was nearly impossible.

Then Leonid threw himself at his legs, looking up at him, demanding his full attention.

He swooped to pick him up, groaning as Leonid's total trust and dependence inundated his heart. He almost succumbed and followed the pattern they'd established, the daily activities that included their quartet—or quintet, with Rosa.

But today would be Caliope's. She'd been here two weeks and had barely seen anything beyond the estate's boundaries. He wanted her to explore his motherland, experience it with him, share a part of him that she hadn't so far. And when she did, she'd make this land a true home for him. Up till now he'd only considered it his birthplace and base of operations.

He looked up from kissing Leonid to find her and his mother gazing at them with their hearts in their eyes, savoring the picture they made together, father and son.

He kissed the top of Leonid's head again. "*Moy dorogoy,* I have to take your *mamochka* on a sightseeing tour that you won't appreciate just yet, so you have to remain here with your *babushka,* Tatjana, and *nyanya,* Rosa, until we come back. But I promise you, tomorrow is all yours, birthday boy."

Caliope's smile faltered. "He can come. I'm sure he'll like it. He likes everything we do together.…"

Khorosho. Good. He'd feared she'd say a point-blank no to the tour. But she only didn't want to leave Leonid behind.

Caliope turned to his mother, and to his hyper senses, there was a hectic tint to her smile. "We can all go. It would a lot of fun with all of us together. I'll go get Rosa."

Ne tak khorosho. Not so good. This was even worse than saying no. She was trying to get out of being alone with him.

Before he could think how to say he wasn't trying to get her alone in front of his mother, said mother intervened.

"I need Rosa while I see to last-minute details of tomorrow's celebration. And you two *will* leave me something to do on my own. And *you,* Caliope, need to see something outside the boundaries of my retreat. Leonid would get bored to tears in tourist attractions and he'd turn your outing into a struggle for all of you." She snapped Leonid out of his arms and almost ran away before Caliope could react, calling across her shoulder over Leonid's gleeful shriek, "Off you go. Shoo."

Caliope gaped after his mother's retreating back for a moment before she turned on him, eyebrow raised.

"You planned this, didn't you?"

His lips spread at her half accusing, half amused expression. "With my mother? No. She's just quick on the uptake. So quick it seems she's been impatiently waiting for me to act your proper host for longer than she could bear."

Her eyes twinkled turquoise with teasing. "If she has been, why didn't she give you a nudge?"

"She's the most progressive mother on the planet and would never interfere in my life. Not that I make it easy for her to be so restrained. My only drawback in her idolizing eyes is my lack of social skills."

She sighed as she fell in step with him. "I used to think so, too. But turns out you're not so bad."

He sighed, too. "I'm trying to recover from a lifelong atrophy of those skills."

"Your recovery has been phenomenal, then. Seems you can't do anything but superlatively."

His heart boomed. He'd become addicted to her praise, when he'd never before cared what anyone thought about him.

Overwhelmed with gratitude that she had forgiven him to the point that she acknowledged his efforts to change for the better, and praised each instance of success, he took her supple hand and raised it to his lips.

At her audible gasp, Maksim immediately broke contact, afraid she'd consider this a breach of their unspoken pact. He couldn't risk spoiling the spontaneity she'd miraculously developed with him.

Pretending an easy smile, he hoped to dissipate tension. "I'm honored by your opinion of my efforts, *moya dorogoya*."

He couldn't stop calling her *my darling*. But she probably thought he meant the milder *my dear,* since he used it with Leonid, too. But they were both his darlings. His only loves.

Still, he kicked himself for succumbing to the need for any physical expression of his emotions when her answering smile wasn't as open as it had previously been. Injecting as much artificial ease into his own, he handed her into his Maserati, then filled her silence with his usual commentary on the areas they were passing through.

At her insistence, after he took her to the major landmarks of the city, he swung by Volkov Iron and Steel Industries headquarters and factories. It felt as if he were seeing it through her eyes, his view of it colored by her appreciation. She told him she'd never seen anything so advanced and extensive. As usual, her approval was what counted most to him.

As the sun started to decline, and while they approached the final man-made attraction he had on his list, she suddenly turned from watching the road to him.

"You haven't told her."

His mother. About the accident. It wasn't a question.

He still answered. "No."

"I'm not prying," she said. "But Mikhail came up yesterday and it was clear she didn't know you were involved in the accident. I just need to know what you told her so I won't say anything wrong if the subject crops up again."

After parking the Maserati, he turned to her, needing to make one thing clear. "You can never pry. It's your right to know anything and everything about me."

Some deeply moved, if stunned emotion swept in her eyes, darkening them.

She didn't already know that she had every right to all of him? Or was it that she didn't want to have that right, since she'd already said she wouldn't take all of him?

He forced himself to smile. "But thanks for your concern. I told her the same story, just took myself out of it. She loved Mikhail as a son, and she suffered his loss almost as much as I did. I just couldn't make it even worse than it is."

"So she doesn't know about…"

It was the first time she'd alluded to his aneurysm, even though she seemed unable to bring herself to name it. That she had brought it up must mean it had been on her mind. As, of *course,* it must have been. Then she held up a hand, asking him not to answer.

But he did. "No, she doesn't know about my…condition."

Her sigh was laden with what sounded like pained relief. "I'm glad you didn't tell her. She's so happy now."

"And it's all thanks to you."

She shook her head. "It's all thanks to Leo."

"And you. I know when my mother is being her usual gracious self and when she is emotionally involved. I can tell she considers you a daughter, not only her grandson's mother."

Those incredible eyes he wanted nothing but to lose himself in gleamed with tears. "Isn't it too early for that?"

"Time has nothing to do with how you feel about someone."

Her slow nod was an admission of how time hadn't factored into what they'd felt about each other from the first moment.

Out loud she only said, "You're right. And I'm glad you think she feels like this, since I feel the same about her. It's the best thing for Leo, to have his family in such accord. I believe he senses it and is thriving on it."

"It's the best thing for you. And for her. You two deserve to have this special connection, regardless of any other consideration, and I can only see it growing deeper by the day." Her nod was ponderous this time, then conceding. To stop himself from swooping on those serious lips, he said, "Now for our last stop in my guided tour, the oldest building in Arkhangel'sk."

In minutes, they were entering the main tower of Gostiny Dvor—The Merchant Court—and Caliope was, as usual, inundating him with questions.

It delighted him how engrossed she was. She already did know a lot about his homeland, as much as could be gleaned from the internet, but she kept asking things only a native would know, to deepen and personalize her knowledge.

He kept answering as they walked through the massive and long complex of buildings. "This place was the raison d'être of Arkhangel'sk in the late seventeenth and eighteenth centuries. During that time, Arkhangel'sk handled more than half the country's exports. As we Russians like our buildings grand, the lofty status of the city back then necessitated building something imposing. It took a team of German and Dutch masons sixteen years to build it. And this turreted trading center was born to become the nexus of all trade between Europe and Russia."

As they entered another section, answering another of her questions had him elaborating on the place's history.

"Yes, everything arrived or left from this network of depots. Luxurious European textiles like satin and velvet were imported, while flax, hemp, wax and timber were exported. But after Peter the Great conquered the Baltic coastline and moved the capital to St. Petersburg, most foreign trade was rerouted and the Arkhangel'sk trade center was abandoned. But by the mid-twentieth century, at the height of communist decay, many of the buildings here followed suit in deterioration and were demolished. After the fall of the Soviet empire in the latter half of the century, the crumbling place was elected to house a local-history museum, but for a long time restoration was never completed due to lack of funds."

"Until you, Arkhangel'sk's archangel, waved your magic wand—" she spread her arms in an encompassing movement "—and restored it to its former and current glory."

He blinked in astonishment. "How do you find these things out? I'm sure they're not on the internet."

She gave him a self-satisfied look. "I have my ways."

Unable to stop, he traced that mischievous dimple on her right cheek. "You have your ways…in everything."

For a long moment, he thought she'd reach up and drag him down for the kiss he knew she was burning for as much as he was.

But she turned away, pretended to look around before returning her gaze to him, with her desire under control. "So are you planning on feeding me, or are you out to make me lose the weight I've put on with Tatjana's mouth-watering feasts?"

Suppressing his own hunger, he fell into step with her as they exited the complex, grinning down at her. "I'm definitely feeding you. There can't be enough of you for me."

Before the heat that flared in her eyes reduced him to ashes, she suppressed it. "There definitely is enough of me, thanks. So take me somewhere with a weight-conscious menu."

He raised an eyebrow at her. "Seafood?"

She burst out laughing. As his other eyebrow joined in his perplexity, she spluttered, "Long story."

On their way to the restaurant, she told him of Aristedes's seafood-related teasing of her during that dinner. He laughed at her account, and they kept laughing all through their meal, about one thing or another. It was amazing how much had changed between them, yet how much remained the same.

They lingered over their meal for hours; then he took her driving outside the city until they reached the nearby Severodvinsk. On its outskirts, he parked the car in the best possible spot, then waited, a smile dancing on his lips in anticipation of Caliope's reaction.

For a while there was none. She was engrossed in discussing Leonid's birthday, expressing her delight that Maksim was flying her family and friends out for the celebration. Then she suddenly stopped and swung her gaze around to stare out of the windshield.

"The aurora!"

His lips spread as she squealed in excitement, sat up straight, eyes wide with wonder, as she, for the first time, witnessed nature's own light show and fireworks.

He watched her as she started swaying with every change in the celestial lights. The glowing curtains undulated as if raining from the heavens in emerald shimmers tinged with cascades of rubies and sapphires and laced with diamonds. They seemed to be dancing to an unheard rhythm, the same one that had caught Caliope and was moving her body with every sweeping arch, with every wave and curl of light moving across the sky, punctuated with sudden rays shooting down from space.

It was a long while before she could tear her eyes from the spectacle. "I've heard how the aurora was spectacular, seen photos and footage of it, but nothing conveyed even one iota of its reality. It's…beyond description."

He nodded, overjoyed at her enthrallment. "That it is. But it's more spectacular than usual tonight. It must have decided to put on an unprecedented show just for you."

She pulled one of those delicious comical faces. "Yeah, sure. It's all on account of the exceptionally clear sky or stronger solar winds…or some other factor."

"Granted, that's the scientific explanation. But why now, and so suddenly? It didn't start showing off until you took notice and started watching."

"Then what are you proposing? That the wavelengths of my delight boosted the magnetic waves causing this phenomenon?"

"Thought waves are electric and magnetic. Why not?"

She pondered his question, her eyes pools reflecting the myriad emissions before she smiled and sighed. "Yeah. Why not? I am enchanted enough to cause it to show off for me."

She sank back in her seat to continue watching the magnificent display, sighed again then suddenly turned to him, face flooding with dismay. "Leo would have loved this! He would have freaked out!"

"It'll still be here for the next three months. We'll bring him another time, after making sure he sleeps during the day so he'll be awake for the show. Tonight I wanted you to relax and enjoy yourself, be yourself, not Leonid's mother."

She relaxed back in her seat, her dainty lips twisting. "You make it sound as if I have no life outside him."

"You only have work. You have no recreation, no fun."

"Look who's talking!"

"I looked, and I didn't like what I saw. Neither of us has to work that hard anymore."

"Who's working hard? I've barely worked since... Well, since you came back. And come to think of it, neither have you."

"I *have* almost ground to a halt for the past three months," he admitted. "But I thought you were working as hard as ever to make up for the times we spent together."

"Are you for real?" She pulled another of those adorable faces. "Apart from the daylong outings and the ton of indoor activities you always plan, it's a miracle I've had time to bathe."

That image of her bathing, the very thing he'd tormented himself with this morning, hit him between the eyes—and in the loins. But the tenderness that she aroused in him was just as fierce. He wanted to give her everything and ensure her fulfillment in every way.

"You only had to tell me I was interfering with your ability to work."

"And what would you have done?" Her eyes gleamed with challenging mischief. "Don't tell me you would have come less frequently for shorter durations. I think it was beyond you to do that. I actually thought it quite a feat that you didn't set up camp in my living room to be with Leo around the clock."

"It wasn't only Leo's side I could barely leave, *moya dorogoya.*" All traces of levity fled at his rasped confession. "But I would have made sure your work never suffered. Don't you know by now that I'll do anything to ensure that you have everything you need, want or aspire to in your life?"

Her eyes became black wells ringed in azure fire as she bit her lower lip, nodded. She knew he meant it.

But did she know *she* meant everything to him?

He opened his mouth to tell her that, that he loved her, worshipped the dirt beneath her feet. But the look in her eyes stopped him. She looked almost…lost. And professing his feelings to her would put her in an even more untenable position.

So he said nothing, just took her hand and leaned back in his seat, pretending to watch the magical manifestation across the sky. Soon she followed suit, and they spent another hour watching in silence until she asked him to take her home.

Maksim stood beneath the stinging, scalding jet of water, willing his senses to subside, his arousal to lessen enough so he wouldn't burst something vital. Like his aneurysm.

Not funny, Volkov. He knew physical stress had nothing to do with the possibility of that ticking bomb in his head going off. If it ever decided to go, it would, just like that. Now it was his heart that might race itself to a standstill.

Caliope had wanted him tonight. He could tell with every fiber of his being that she'd been craving him from that first night. But tonight, being alone and free from distractions, her hunger had almost killed him. Up till the moment they'd parted ways in the hallway.

If he pushed, if he went to her now, snatched her up into his arms and marched back to his suite, he knew she'd go up in flames in his arms. She'd beg him to take her, plunder her to sobbing, nerveless satiation.

But he couldn't. It wouldn't mean anything if she didn't seek him as she once had, out of her own free will and full choice. So though he craved her desperately, would do just about anything to have her, he couldn't take her power away like that.

Which meant he'd live in hell for the rest of his miserable life—one that he could only pray would be long, for Leonid's sake—and try to find a way to withstand the torture of her nearness.

It was no use now. His body remained clenched under the unremitting barrage of yearning that neither punishingly hot nor cold water had ameliorated. He rinsed the hair she'd told him she loved long, combed it back out of his eyes with his fingers, reliving the times she'd done that, until he couldn't bear the phantom sensations of her hands running through…

"Maksim."

He squeezed his eyes tighter. He kept hearing her voice calling him. As she used to—intimate, hot, hungry.

"Maksim."

There he went again. But this time, it sounded so…real.

Knowing he'd kick himself for being a wishful fool, his eyes snapped open to make certain. And through the heavy spray and the misted glass of the cubicle…there she was. *Caliope.*

As if from the depth of a dream, he pushed the door open.

And she was really there. Standing framed against the closed, ivory-painted door in a satin-and-lace nightgown and robe a darker shade of her eyes, just like he'd imagined in his fantasies.

His senses rioted so violently, he almost charged her. But he had to wait for her to tell him what she wanted.

For soul-searing moments she stared at him, her eyes briefly leaving his to skim over his body, wincing as she saw the evidence of his accident in his fading scars, then gasping at the sight of his arousal, before returning to his face.

He could barely hear her whisper over the still-pounding shower. "I couldn't wait any longer."

Then she moved, strode toward him, picking up speed with every urgent step. With the last one she threw herself against him under the gushing spray of water.

He almost lost his balance with her hurtling momentum and barely steadied them, looked down at her in pure astonishment. Was this really happening?

In answer to his silent disbelief, she climbed him, winding herself around him, twisting in his arms, forcing him to press her against the marble wall.

His hand behind her head and his arm at her back took the impact at the last second. They remained like this for endless moments, panting, their bodies and gazes fused. And he saw it all written all over her face, in the depths of her eyes: memories, longing, hunger…everything.

Then her hands were stabbing into his hair as he'd been yearning for them to minutes ago, grabbing his head by its tether and dragging his lips down to hers. She wrenched at them, and when he only surrendered to her fervor, paralyzed under the onslaught of her feel, the disbelief at her actions, she whimpered in frustration, bit his lower lip, hard.

A guttural growl rumbled from his gut as he dropped her to her feet and tore the clinging wet ensemble off her body. Then she was naked against him. She crushed her swollen, hard-tipped breasts against his chest, rubbed her firm belly feverishly against his steel erection.

Before his mind overloaded, he dropped to his knee to rid her of her last barrier, that wisp of turquoise lace. But as he started worshipping the feast of her long-craved flesh, her hands were again gripping his hair, pulling him back up to his feet. Straining against him, climbing him again, trembling all over now, she clamped her legs around his buttocks and sobbed, streams of tears flowing with the water sluicing over her face.

"I need you inside me…now, Maksim, *now.*"

"Caliope, *moya serdtse…*"

He didn't recognize the voice of the beast who'd growled this to her, proclaiming her his heart. He was abruptly at the end of his tether, no more finesse, no more restraint. She'd demolished his control with her distressed demand.

Fusing their mouths together, he flexed his hips, his manhood nudging her entrance, and went blind with the sledgehammer of pleasure as her hot and molten core opened for him. Passion roared as she surrendered fully, all of her shuddering apart for his invasion, his completion.

But as he began to ease himself inside her, she bit down hard on his lip again. "I can't *bear* slow or gentle. Give me all you have, all your strength and greed. Devastate me, *finish* me."

He would have withheld his next heartbeats than deny her what she needed. Holding her gaze that shimmered with tears, he stabbed his girth inside her, hard and fierce. Her hot, honeyed flesh yielded to his invasion as he watched greedily the shocked wonder and pained pleasure slashing across her magnificent face, squeezing out of her in splintering, ravenous cries.

He bottomed out in her depths with that first ferocious plunge, dropped his forehead to hers, groaned deep and long at the severity of sensations. "Caliope, at last, *moya dusha,* at last…"

"Yes…Maksim, do it, take everything, do it all to me. I missed you so much, I've gone insane missing you.…"

Unable to hold back anymore, he rammed into her, that unbearable tightness still the same sheath of madness he remembered, even after she'd given him Leonid. The impossible fit, the end of his exile, coming home inside her, sent him out of his mind. He withdrew and rammed back again and again, turning her cries to squeals, then shrieks.

She thrashed against him as her slick flesh clamped around his length with a force he was only too familiar with, had craved to insanity. The herald of her orgasm. He knew what it would take now to give her an explosive release, wring her voluptuous body of every last spark of sensation and satisfaction.

He built the momentum of his thrusts until he was jackhammering inside her in frantic, forceful jabs. Her convulsions started from the farthest point he plunged, constricting her whole body around him, inside and out. Her shrieks became one continuous scream, stifling as bursts of completion raged through her.

He withstood her storm until she'd expended every shudder and tear, then he finished her as she'd always craved him to, impaling her beyond her limits, nudging the very core of her femininity, releasing his agonized ecstasy there, in one burst after another of scorching pleasure.

She sagged in his arms, nerveless, replete. He, too, could barely stand, so sank down, containing her. It felt as if she had been made to fit within him, as if he had been made to wrap around her.

His mind was a total blank as his tongue mated with hers in a languid, healing duel. He'd thought he'd starved for her taste. He'd been wrong. He'd shriveled up and expired. Drinking from its very fount was a resurrection.

A long, long time later, he relinquished her lips to gaze down at her. Her head fell back against his shoulder, her eyes drugged with satisfaction.

Then those lips he'd kissed swollen moved, and that beloved voice poured out in a heartbreakingly tender melody.

Then he realized what she'd said.

"Will you marry me, Maksim?"

Eight

Maksim stared at Caliope's flushed face and intoxicated eyes and wondered if his mind had finally snapped.

If he'd been able to think at all about what her coming to him meant, he wouldn't have dared to hope for more than her finally accepting him as a lover again. So he couldn't be hearing what he wanted to hear. Since he hadn't wanted to hear *that*.

This meant…this was real. She meant it.

One question expanded to fill the world. But he couldn't ask it just yet. He had to take her out of here.

Coordination shot from the one-two combo of satiation and shock, he turned the water off, then scooped her up. He stepped with his armful of replete woman outside the shower, dried her then carried her to bed. She surrendered to his ministrations like a feline delighting in her owner's cosseting.

Coming down beside her on the bed, entwining their nakedness, sweeping her beloved flesh in caresses and her face in kisses, he asked the one thing left in his mind.

"Why? What changed?"

She pulled back to stare into his eyes. And the change in hers startled him. They looked somber, sorrowful.

"Don't…*bozhe moy,* please don't. I can't bear you to feel a moment's distress. I don't need explanations. I don't need to know anything more than that you're here in my arms."

She cupped his face in her hands, her eyes beseeching. "But I need you to understand why I said no, why I held you at arm's length the past three months." She paused, inhaled a shuddering breath. "It was because of Leonidas."

Her dead brother, the one she'd named Leonid after.

Feeling her revelations would hurt her, he didn't want her to go on. But he also sensed that she needed to unburden herself. He turned his lips into the palm caressing his face and nodded, encouraging her to continue.

She did, sharing with him the intensely personal loss for the first time. "I never told you much about what happened, because we didn't delve into each other's private lives before, then because it remained too painful even when we did. Leonidas was…was the closest to me in age, and in everything. My only friend. My Mikhail." He ran soothing hands down her back, fortifying her when she faltered. She went on, her voice subdued. "He, too, was into extreme sports, though the extreme exertion variety. He was competing in a decathlon when he suffered a severe fracture in his left knee. During treatment, it was discovered the fracture had tumors behind them, in his tibia and femur around the joint—what he'd long thought was overtraining pain. After investigation, it was found to be an extremely malignant form of osteosarcoma."

His heart convulsed. He now knew where this was probably going. He hugged her closer, as if to ward off the desperation she'd felt for the sibling she'd loved most in the world.

"We told everyone his surgery was to fix his fracture. Only I knew it was a tumor-resection, limb-salvage surgery. But he was already in an advanced stage with metastasis to the lungs. We were told with aggressive treatments he had about fifty percent chance of survival. I talked him into going for it, since he was otherwise healthy and could withstand treatment, and I'd be there with him every step of the way. He agreed and I moved in with him, and we went through the cycles of treatment, which he weathered as best as could be expected."

Her eyes started to overflow with remembered despair, her whole body buzzing with the desolation of reliving the ordeal. "But a year later, another tumor was found, and this time there would have been no way to salvage his leg. And his survival rates had also plummeted. As we left the hospital, he told me he wanted to be on his own for a while, would come home later. But in two hours, I was contacted by the police. He'd just had a fatal car crash."

It was agonizing to see the shock in her eyes as if it was fresh, as if she relived the loss all over again.

"I...I thought I had more time with him. But he was suddenly gone, and everything I'd been bottling up since the discovery of his cancer and during his agonizing treatments—the pain, the fear, the constant anxiety—came crashing down on me. It was such a devastating blow, knowing it had all been for nothing. For months I didn't know that I'd ever rise from beneath the rubble. Then I met you."

When she'd detailed the emotional abuse her mother had gone though at the hands of the father she'd never seen, he'd thought this explained her no-strings-attached position on intimacy when they'd met. But this revelation gave a far deeper dimension to her mindset at the time. She'd met him in the aftermath of this life-changing loss, must have been reeling, needing closeness yet dreading it.

Remorse tore into him again, fiercer than ever before. "And I exposed you to more distress, especially when I deserted you, and then came back offering you more angst and uncertainty."

Her tears abruptly stopping, a look of urgency and con-

viction replaced the despondency on her beloved face.
"No, Maksim. I see now that your problems did seem insurmountable to you back then, and I no longer think telling me about your past at the time would have led to us
working things out. We both had to go through all this to
know ourselves better, and to find out what we mean to
each other, for better or for worse."

Still feeling unworthy of her love and forgiveness, after
all that he'd put her through, he pulled away and sat up.
"I understood why you said no to my proposal. I was too
much of a risk, on every front, and you had your priorities right. But I didn't imagine you had such personal injury and dread to fortify your rejection. Now that I know,
I can't understand why you've suddenly changed your
mind about us."

She sat up, too, a goddess of voluptuousness, her breasts
full and lush, her waist nipped, her thighs long and sleek,
her hair gleaming silk around her polished shoulders. His
body roared, forcing him to snatch the covers to hide his
engorged erection, angry at his reaction when he should
be tending to her emotional needs.

But she pressed her softness into his hardness, palm
spreading over his heart, turning arousal to distress.

"There's nothing sudden about it," she murmured
against his chest. "I refused you that first night because I
thought I could go back to my old life, raising Leo alone
without you. But I couldn't act on my conviction and I
let you in, and there's no changing that you are part of
our family, part of *us*, now. *Ya lyublyu tebya...nye magoo
zheet byes tebya....* I love you and I can't live without you,
Maksim. So will you marry me, *moy lyubov?* You've already claimed me as yours."

Hearing her calling him her love, admitting his claim
to her heart, her life, was beyond endurance.

What had he done?

He had craved her nearness and passion, but he hadn't thought she'd open herself so completely to him like this. He'd only ever wanted the best for her, and Leo.

"What if you were right to refuse me? What if the worst thing that ever happened to you is when I insinuated myself into your lives? What if something happens to me…?"

She stemmed the flow of his doubts and trepidations in a desperate kiss. "I already loved you with everything in me *before* you left. It was why your departure devastated me. And I've loved you more with each moment since your return. If anything happens to you now, whether we're married or not, it would shatter me just the same. So really, all I've been achieving by keeping you away is depriving us of all the intimacy only we can give each other, and having the pain without the pleasure."

His whole body stiffened as if under a barrage of blows. To imagine her in pain was unendurable. He'd wanted to love her, but he hadn't wanted her to suffer the agony of loving him to the same degree, to live in fear for him.

As if realizing the trajectory of his thoughts, she tugged on his hair to bring him out of his surrender to recriminations. "As you said that first night—nobody knows how long they'll live, or how long they'll have with someone. All we can do as finite humans is take whatever we can whenever we can and make the best of it. And you are the best possible *everything* that has ever happened to me. You're also the best father I've seen or imagined, surpassing even Aristedes."

The delight of her adulation, the dread of her dependence, sank into his heart with joy and terror.

But he'd created this impossible dilemma. She already loved him as much as he loved her, and he would hurt her whether he gave her the closeness and commitment she now craved or if he maintained their status quo. He'd been a fool not to realize how risky this all was, to think they could share so much without dragging her down into the well of addiction with him. He'd done this to her, and could only now give her whatever she wanted. Every single second of his life, every spark of his being.

What she already had total claim to.

Now she needed his corroboration. And for him to provide a distraction from all this overwrought emotion.

He forced a grin to his lips. "Better than the legendary Aristedes, huh? And you're not biased at all, of course."

An impish grin overlapped her urgency, transforming her face. "Not one tiny bit. He's a close second, granted, but you're the unapproachable number one." She pushed him on his back, coming to lie on top of him, pressing her hot length to his every inch. "So since it would be for better or for worse between us from now on, whether I marry you or not, 'not' is only pointless denial. So I again ask you, *moy serdtse*. Marry me."

He gazed up at her adoringly, unable to do anything anymore but risk living with constant worry and dread for the pleasure and privilege of any time they could have together.

"*Pozhaluista, moy lyubov*... Please, my love, say yes."

How could he say anything else? "Yes, *moy dusha*, yes.… I'm all yours to do with as you please."

He rose beneath her and swept her around until he was pressing down on her between her eagerly spreading legs.

Tears of happiness glittered as she arched, opening herself for his domination. "As soon as possible?"

"How about tomorrow?" He delivered the words into her lips as he thrust inside her, going home.

The shock of his combined proposition and invasion tore a cry from her depths.

With ecstasy shuddering across her face, she wrapped herself around him, taking him deeper, and moaned, "Yes."

Caliope still couldn't believe it.

She'd gone to Maksim's room last night without thinking.

She'd just been unable to stay away anymore. None of what had happened—their intimacies, her confessions, her proposal—had been in the least premeditated. Not only hadn't she thought of impassioned arguments to convince him to marry her beforehand, she hadn't even first convinced *herself*. She'd just gone to him, and had taken this life-altering step.

But then her fate had changed forever the moment she'd met his eyes across that reception hall three years ago. There'd always been no going back. The only difference now was that she was finally at peace with it, wouldn't settle for anything less.

If she couldn't be with him, she wanted nothing at all.

She passed by one of the ornate mirrors studding the walls of the mansion and met her own eyes. And winced.

Could it be more obvious that she'd barely survived a night of wild possession with that incomparable Russian wolf?

Everything about her was sore and swollen; even her hips swayed in a way that said she'd been plundered. As she'd begged him to when he'd attempted gentleness. She'd wanted him to dominate and devastate her. And how he had.

They hadn't slept at all, but who needed sleep? The rush of his lovemaking would keep her awake and going for a week straight. She felt as energized and as alert as she'd ever been. But it had only been after making love to her for the fifth time that they'd finally taken a breath not laden with delirium, and she'd started having qualms about saying yes to his proposition of an immediate wedding.

Fearing their anniversary would be supplanted by Leo's birthday, she'd proposed they keep their guests here for a few days and then have their wedding at the end of the week.

But he'd insisted that they didn't need a specific date every year to celebrate their marriage, since he'd be celebrating with her every single day. And she'd believed him.

So they were having their wedding today.

At 6:00 a.m. sharp, he'd gone to prepare everything and she'd given him carte blanche to do whatever he saw fit. She had no demands, only wanted to have the freedom of showing him that he was her everything. And to announce their bond to the world.

She'd seen tears fill his eyes before. But last night, they'd flowed. Hers had flooded in response, then deluged when he'd asked *her* to tell the world, starting with his mother.

He wanted her to be the one to give his mother what he knew would be the best gift anyone could give her, after that of Leo. A wife for her son. A daughter-in-law. A daughter, period.

And she had a six-thirty meeting with Tatjana at the chamber where they'd planned on holding Leo's birthday party, and where they'd now also have their wedding. Leo had practically been the one to pick the setting in the dance hall or "hall of mirrors". His delight in its painted ceilings and ornate, mirror-covered walls had been so explicit, he'd had them stay there at least an hour a day, as he pranced on top of tables in front of the mirrors, turned upside down to see himself from all different angles and rolled on the ground to stare at the ceiling. It was also the setting for a most important milestone. He'd taken his first steps there a couple of days after they'd arrived in Arkhangel'sk.

He'd chosen well, since it was the mansion's largest and most decorated room. But with the list of people Tatjana had invited, seemingly all the citizens of Arkhangel'sk, they'd need more than that space. Maybe even *all* of the mansion.

Her feet almost leaving the ground, she rushed through said mansion, feeling again as if she'd stepped back in time, all the time half expecting she'd meet figures from the era of the tsars.

It almost seemed an anachronism that the people she did meet, those who worked on the estate and on Tatjana's myriad community projects—all part of her continuous efforts to act as the community's uncrowned queen—were all jarringly modern.

She smiled left and right to everyone she met, almost running the last steps as she entered the dance hall.

The sight that greeted her had her heart doing its usual jig. Tatjana and Leo were perfect together. She was grateful every minute she'd agreed to come here, to give them all this rich and unique relationship. Rosa, an integral part of the family now, was also having the time of her life here, and apparently finding the love of her life, too, in Sasha, Maksim's chauffeur/bodyguard.

Could things get more perfect?

As soon as she thought that, her heart quivered with trepidation.

Could anything be this perfect…for long?

"Caliope, *moya dorogoya!*"

Tatjana's cheerfulness jerked her out of those dark thoughts, and she ran to her and to Leo.

For the next fifteen minutes, Tatjana didn't give her the chance to say much of anything as she supplied her

with every minute detail of the birthday-party preparations, then solicited her opinion on changes in the color
schemes, menu and seating plans.

Leo soon got bored, and Rosa took him away to what
Maksim had transformed into every child's wonderland.

Then Tatjana was sweeping her along to her favorite
sitting place, the grand living room. It was studded with
paintings and decorations that felt like a documentary of
the long history and glory of the Volkov family. Something Maksim had never mentioned.

As much as he was copious with his information about
the country and the region, he'd been stingy with family
details.

From what he'd told her of his father and grandfather,
she understood his reluctance. She'd at first thought it
wasn't a good idea to know more than she already knew.
But now she felt she needed to glean as much information
as possible in order to know him from every facet. She'd
tried to broach the subject many times, but he'd always
ingeniously escaped giving any details.

But here she was, with the one other person who could
supply her with the knowledge she needed. Not that she
had one single idea how to introduce the topic. If she asked
outright, it would appear as if she was prying into mat-
ters Maksim hadn't seen fit to share with her. Which, of
course, she was.

But what was she *thinking?* She should be telling Tatjana of the wedding, not trying to get her to spill the
Volkov family secrets!

Tatjana offered her a plate of *pirozhki,* mouthwatering
pastries filled with potato and cheese, with a side bowl
of *smetana,* delicious sour cream that Russians used co-
piously.

Cali reciprocated by handing her tea, then began, "Tatjana…"

Clearly not realizing that she was cutting her off, Tatjana said, "Maksim didn't tell you much about his father, did he? Or about my marriage to him? Beside it being an abusive relationship that ended horrifically?"

Whoa. Had she been thinking of it so intensely she'd telepathically conveyed her burning curiosity to Tatjana?

She could only shake her head.

Tatjana sighed. "It pains me that he can't forgive or forget."

Cali put down the *pirozhki,* suddenly finding eating impossible. "Is it conceivable to do either when such wrongs have been dealt? I wondered how you survived when he first told me. But now that I've seen you, I know you're the strongest person I've ever known, and you can weather anything. And from the way you talk about your late husband, I can sense that *you,* at least, have forgiven him. And I wonder how you did it."

"I want to tell you how so you can understand Maksim better. But I have to tell you my life story to explain."

Cali nodded, even the slight movement difficult.

Tatjana sighed again. "I first saw Grigori when I was twenty and he was twenty-nine. I was working in one of the timber factories here when he came with his father, the city's governor, to learn the ropes of the position he would occupy, which would place him on his father's and grandfather's paths, as high-ranking Soviet officials. I was struck by him, and he was as struck by me."

She paused for a brief moment before continuing. "But all talk of equality in communism aside, a poor factory worker and a young man from what was considered the new royalty in Soviet Russia was an impossible proposition. But he moved heaven and earth, and fought his father and family long and hard to have me. Though I was at times disturbed by his intensity, I was hopelessly attracted to him. And he did seem like a fairy tale come true to the girl I was then."

She took a sip of tea, encouraged Cali to do the same. Cali gulped down a scalding mouthful, on the edge of her seat, the feeling that she'd plunged into a past life and another era intensifying.

Tatjana went on. "Then we were married. But for years, I couldn't conceive. Everyone kept pushing him to leave me, as not only was I inappropriate but barren. I think he thought it was him who was barren, and he grew progressively more morose, especially as his positions kept getting bigger and his responsibilities with them. It was five years after we got married that I became pregnant. I think he always had unreasonable doubts that Maksim wasn't his."

Was that what had driven him to abuse his wife and son? He'd believed she'd betrayed him to conceive, then saddled him with the fruit of her infidelity to raise as his own?

"Not that his abuse started only then. It just started to become a pattern." So much for that theory. The bastard had already been an unstable monster. "But it was a terrible time all around. We were passing through the worst phases of the Cold War, and the situation of almost everyone in Russia was dismal. Having a husband who slapped me around, but otherwise gave me, and my family, everything, seemed like such a tiny quibble in comparison to those who had no homes or jobs or food. And I was inexperienced for my age, having been totally sheltered living here, so I didn't know any better."

Just like Cali's mother. It made her again realize just how much women today took for granted in all the rights and powers they'd gained in the past fifty years.

"After the birth of Maksim, Grigori was promoted to become the vice governor, a position he soon realized he was totally unsuited for. But he couldn't admit that or risk dishonoring his father—and himself—forever. He knew what happened to those they considered inadequate in the hierarchy. He struggled, and it only got worse as time went by. Reports of his mistakes and investigations into his failures began to accumulate, and he began to disintegrate."

Cali had to bite her tongue. If the older woman thought she'd make her sympathize with the weak bastard who'd scarred Maksim, and almost had made him destroy what they'd had and had now regained by a sheer miracle, she had another think coming!

Unaware of her venom, Tatjana went on. "He started to take it out on me more often, but as Maksim grew bigger and began to stand up for me and antagonize him for what he did to me, he turned his wrath on him. I believe he was more convinced every day that Maksim couldn't hate him like that if he was his. Then, in spite of all my measures, I got pregnant again. I thought of terminating the pregnancy, but ultimately didn't have the heart to and was forced to tell Grigori. His paranoia increased, but he didn't fully break down until he was fired from his position, just five months after Ana was born. We were given a month's notice to vacate this residence for his replacement. On the day we were set to leave, he went berserk, accusing me of being the reason for all his ill fortune, that I blighted him with my two bastards and…the rest you know."

Oh, she knew. And now hated Maksim's father all the more. Try as she might, she just couldn't understand how Tatjana managed to remain this adjusted, considering everything she'd endured.

Tatjana sighed. "Now comes the part about me and Maksim. We came out of the hospital to find no home and no family, as my parents had died and I had no siblings, and Grigori's family wanted nothing to do with us. He'd made a lot of enemies here and so much of his failures were snowballing." She sighed again, remembered sadness tingeing her face. "The whole place seemed to be going to hell. I worked any job I could find, and my darling Maksim was with me every step of the way, studying, working, doing everything for me that grown men couldn't. I don't think I would have survived without him.

"Then the Soviet Union collapsed and it was mayhem for a long while. I was almost afraid Maksim had turned to crime when he kept coming home covered in cuts and bruises. But he was actually defending the helpless here against the criminals who were exploiting them. And instead of working in a job in the industries here, he wanted to introduce something new to the region, so he could rule it. He chose steel. But he needed to learn the process from the ground up, so we went to Magnitogorsk, the center of steel industries in Russia. He made a living for us right away, then kept soaring higher every day. By the time he was in his mid-twenties, he'd already become a millionaire. He took us back here to set up Volkov Iron and Steel Industries and bought me this place."

Caliope had given up trying to hold back the tears. Imagining Maksim as a young boy, then teenager, then young man, as he struggled through the most unforgiving of social, political and financial circumstances, fending for his mother and all who needed his superior courage and strength and intellect, surmounting any difficulties and coming out not only on top but as such a phenomenal success, was beyond awe inspiring.

To think he was hers was still unbelievable.

But another thing was incomprehensible. "Why did

you want to reclaim the place where you'd both suffered so much?"

Tatjana's eyes, which were so much like Maksim's, melted with tenderness. "Because my main memories here consisted of being with my beloved son. And my parents until they died. And after the loss and the pain began to fade away, I needed those precious memories back."

"But what about Maksim?" Cali said. "Doesn't your staying here make it hard for him to spend time with you?"

"I do know that the good memories with me don't make up for the horrible ones for him. But it's not only family nostalgia that made me wish to be back here. I have a responsibility to the people here, who stood by me at my worst times, and whom Grigori's mismanagement had harmed. I wanted to provide as many jobs and do my part in developing the community on a cultural and social level as Maksim was doing on an economic one."

This explained so much. Everything, really. She now finally and fully understood how he'd become the man she loved and respected with all her soul.

And now it was time to give Tatjana the wonderful news.

But Tatjana wasn't finished. She put her cup down and reached for both of Cali's hands, her eyes solemn. "I know Maksim always carried within him the fear that he might manifest his father's instability, but I assure you, Caliope, Maksim is nothing like his father or his menfolk. He'd been tested in the crucible of unendurable tests and had remained in control and never exhibited his father's volatility, not for a moment. In fact, he becomes more stable under pressure." Fierce maternal faith crossed Tatjana's face and her voice filled with urgency. "So you have absolutely *nothing* to fear. Maksim would rather die than raise a hand against anyone weaker, let alone those whom he loves and who depend on him."

Cali was the one who squeezed Tatjana's hands now, soothing her agitation. "I know that, Tatjana. I'm certain of it as much I'm certain that I'm alive."

"Then why won't you marry him?" Tatjana cried.

So that was what this was all about? Her future mother-in-law selling her on the idea of marrying her son?

Joy fizzed in her blood as her lips split in a grin that must have blinded Tatjana.

"Who said I won't? I'm marrying him…today!"

Nine

After announcing to Tatjana the wedding would be that very same day, and after the older woman had gotten over her *very* vocal shock, she hadn't even attempted to talk her into a postponement to give them time to prepare. According to Maksim's mother, this was three years overdue and they weren't putting it off one second longer. And then they still had twelve hours. *Plenty* of time in the hands of someone versed in preparing celebrations.

Of that Cali was sure. Between Maksim and his mother, who'd each separately promised her a wedding to rival those of the tsars, she knew they could make anything come true.

Not that she cared about what the wedding would be like. She only wanted her family and friends here to see her exchange vows with Maksim, even in her current jeans and ponytail if need be. All that truly mattered was becoming Caliope Volkov...

Caliope Volkov. She liked that. No. She *loved* that. And she loved that Leo would become Leonidas Maksim Volkov. His doting father had said he'd grow into a fearsome man, both lion and wolf.

Though she was considering changing Leo's name to Leonid, as Maksim called him. To give tribute to Leonidas yet at the same time pay proper homage to Leo's heritage. Maksim had refused that categorically, saying that he'd stop calling him Leonid if she thought he preferred it, that he just found it more natural to say. He wanted her to honor her brother and best friend, and was honored that she'd named his son after him.

When they couldn't reach a compromise, he'd suggested they leave it up to Leo to choose when he grew older.

Not that this was a time to think of names. Now it was time to be swept into the whirlwind of preparations.

"So your man is so stingy, he wants to squeeze one major and another monumental event into one?"

Cali rushed out of the bathroom at hearing the deep teasing voice, squealing in pleasure at finding Aristedes and Selene and their two kids standing on her suite's doorstep.

Though she was already so tired all she wanted was to collapse in bed and snooze for ten hours straight, she hurtled herself at the quartet, deluging them with hugs and kisses.

As she carried Sofia and cooed to her how her auntie had missed her and how her cousin Leo couldn't wait to have someone his age around, Aristedes continued his mockery.

"I've heard of double birthdays or weddings, but a baby birthday and the wedding of said baby's parents? That's new."

Selene nipped his chin in tender chastisement. "You are *not* going to start playing the nitpicking brother-in-law."

Aristedes turned indulgent eyes to his wife. "That's my kid sister over here. You bet I'm going to watch that Russian wolf's every breath and hold him accountable for her every smile. And if I see as much as one tear…"

Selene curled her lips at him. "You mean like the rivers you made me cry once?"

He narrowed his eyes, clearly still disturbed that he'd caused her pain for any reason. "That was before we married."

Selene arched one elegant, dark eyebrow at him. "And now you're walking the line because I have not one but three hulking, overbearing Greek brothers watching your every breath and holding you accountable for my every smile."

"If you think those brothers of yours have *any*..."

"Down, Aris." Selene dragged him down for a laughing kiss. "That was just me teasing you to make you lay off Maksim." At his harrumph, which said he took severe exception to any allusions—if even in jest—that her brothers could *ever* influence his behavior, especially concerning her, she turned to wink at Cali. "He still has humorless blackouts. But I'm working on him."

"You've done a miraculous job so far." Cali giggled, fiercely happy to see how adored her eldest brother was by the woman who owned his heart. "Before you, we didn't think he had humor installed at all. We didn't think he was human!"

"Like your man, you mean?" Aristedes twisted his lips, hugging Selene more securely, his eyes darting to keep track of Alex, who'd climbed Cali's bed and was playing with the articles on her nightstand. "He was established as an arctic Russian robot of the highest order."

Selene chuckled. "Seems we'll discover that your man and mine are twins separated at birth."

Cali burst out laughing. "Just substitute Russian for Greek and anything you say about one could well be describing the other."

Aristedes pursed his lips, not quite mockingly this time.

"Good news for your man is he finally did the right thing. And he wore you down in record time, too."

"You're wrong on both counts, since I was the one who asked him to marry me, and three months felt like forever."

A lethal bolt of lightning burst in Aristedes's steel eyes. "You mean you were the one trying to pin him down to a commitment all this time?"

She held up a placating hand. "First, 'down, Aris,' like Selene just said. Second, there is no pinning down involved. We both want this with every fiber of our beings. Third, he asked me to marry him the first night he came back and I turned him down, but he proceeded to dedicate his life to me and Leo anyway. Then just yesterday, I faced it that we have no life without him. But knowing he'd never ask again, so he wouldn't pressure me, I had to propose this time."

Still looking unconvinced, Aristedes growled under his breath. "This had better be the truth, Cali."

Did he suspect she had their mother's victim affliction? The very thing their sisters had, to one degree or another?

She held his eyes reassuringly. "It is. I don't have a blind-eye-turning bone in my body."

His eyes bored into hers as it to gauge the veracity of her claim. Then he inhaled. "As long as you're sure…"

"I am." She handed him Sofia, who'd nestled into her neck and gone to sleep, and ran to fetch Alex. Once she had him carrying both of his children, she turned him around toward the door. "Now I'll borrow your wife and you go fetch me Melina, Phaidra, Thea and Kassandra, too."

"You called?"

The cheerful voice was Thea's. The next second, she had appeared in the doorway, followed by everyone Cali had just named. They were all wearing the same dress that was sculpted over Selene—an incredible sleeveless creation with an off-shoulder décolletage, nipped waist and flowing skirt in powder-blue, supple satin embroidered with gold thread. Which meant they were serving as her bridesmaids. The ever-present lump in her throat expanded.

"How's that for fast service?" Kassandra chuckled.

"You're mind readers." Cali pounced on them and dragged them in, before turning back to Aristedes. "You go see what Maksim has planned for you during the ceremony, but behave or I'll sic Selene on you." Aristedes gave a sigh of mock resignation, dropping a kiss on her cheek, then another on Selene's lips.

Before he walked away, she clung to him. "Is he here?"

His lips thinned. "Andreas? I would have skinned him alive if he didn't come."

She winced. "You have a thing for skinning alive men who don't perform to your standards, don't you?"

He exhaled. "Lucky for him, I won't have to this time. He wasn't coming when it was only Leo's birthday, but as per his words, 'not even a bastard like him would miss his kid sister's wedding.'"

Not exactly the enthusiasm she would have hoped for from her older brother, but all that mattered was that Andreas was here. Everyone was here.

Her eyes filled, her chest tightened. As it seemed was her natural state these days.

Aristedes kissed her again. "Now hurry and be a ready bride so I can give you away. And ladies, don't get so carried away dressing her up that you lose track of time and keep us waiting too long."

"We don't *have* long," Cali wailed as she closed the door to drown out the sound of his infuriating chuckling, then turned to the grinning women. "Wait until you see what Maksim sent me for a wedding dress. I'm afraid to even…approach the thing, let alone wear it. And to think I sent away those stylists and beauticians Maksim hired to help me get ready, thinking I can manage."

Selene smiled. "Based on his similarity to Aris, I bet he has them standing by in case you change your mind."

"He did send in plan B." Melina pointed at herself.

Phaidra nodded. "Yep. He barely saluted us before almost chasing us here so we'd run to tend to your needs."

"But what were you thinking sending professionals away, you silly girl?" Thea scolded. "Since when do you know the first thing about makeup and hairdressing, when you never use any with your disgustingly perfect coloring and hair?"

Cali sighed as they approached the dressing room. "Your all-too-kind compliments aside, that's why I didn't want their services. Makeup and a hairdo would make me look different, and I don't want Maksim to find a woman he doesn't know walking down the aisle to him. Then I saw the so-called wedding dress and its accessories and almost fainted. Here…" She turned on the dressing room's lights. "You'll see what I mean."

Everyone blinked and their jaws dropped.

But it was Kassandra, of course, who recognized what that masterpiece was.

Her exclamation reverberated in the spacious room. "That's Empress Alexandra Feodorovna's dress!"

Yep. Maksim had gotten her the dress of the freaking last tsarina of Russia. She'd recognized it from her extensive research into his motherland's history.

Kassandra shook her head in disbelief. "It has to be a replica. That V-shaped satin inlay in the bodice below the embroidery was red in the original. This one's is—" she swung her dazed gaze to Cali "—the exact color of your eyes."

Cali's eyes misted again at the lengths he'd gone to at such short notice. "I thought so at first, but couldn't figure out how he could have had a replica made in under ten hours. The more plausible, if more insane, explanation is that he had the original customized to me."

"But…but—he couldn't have!" Kassandra looked faint with even imagining this. This would be tantamount to sacrilege to the designer in her. "That dress, if it's the real thing, is a…a *relic*. He couldn't have tampered with it for any reason. And how could he have gotten his hands on it at all? God, Cali, just *who* is this man you're marrying?"

"A very, *very* influential man, m'dear," Selene retorted.

But Kassandra was rushing to closely examine the dress in openmouthed shock and wonder and was joined by the others.

Selene remained beside Cali. "For your ears only, Cali, since the ladies are overwhelmed enough, I wouldn't put obtaining such an artifact past Maksim. Literally anything is possible with our one-in-a-billion men."

Kassandra turned stricken eyes to them. "It's done ingeniously, but I can detect where the azure inlay overlies the original red. It is *the* dress."

Cali shuddered. "So I was right to fear touching it."

Thea scratched her head. "Apart from its pricelessness, how do you put it on? I don't see any zippers or buttons."

"It does seem as if there is no way to get into it," Phaidra agreed.

"Oh, of course there is." Kassandra waved their stymied perplexity away with the assurance of an expert. "And it's a good thing you declined putting on makeup, Cali. I would have had an ulcer dreading you'd smudge this one-in-history masterpiece." She picked up the extremely heavy dress reverently, her eyes eating up the details before turning to the others. "You ladies sit down over there—" she indicated the brocade couches on the other side of the room "—while I get Cali into this, and we'll get this show on the road."

Selene curtsied. "You're the boss here, Kass."

Melina bowed before Kassandra with arms stretched in mock worship. "She is the goddess, you mean. She conjured those bridesmaid's dresses in Maksim's demanded shade for all of us in under three hours!"

Imitating their sister, Thea and Phaidra bowed to Kassandra, who touched their gleaming heads in mock magnanimity, before they all burst out laughing.

Sobering a bit, Kassandra said, "Seriously, I couldn't have gotten everything done on *that* short a notice. I made the final selections, but it was Maksim's magic wand that had the dresses adjusted and flown in to your doorsteps in time."

As Cali's eyes welled and her sisters swooned over her groom's gallantry, Kassandra shooed them away again.

Clearly delighted to not have to handle Cali's wedding artifact, to sit down and watch as if they were in a fashion show, everyone hurried to comply with Kassandra's directives while Cali rushed after her to the changing room.

Ten minutes later, she stood gaping at herself. It was a good thing she'd declined a professional hairdo and makeup. With only the dress, she looked totally transformed. The white satin masterpiece molded to her like an extension of her. The bodice opened on a plunging off-the-shoulders oval décolleté, pointing into a sharp V at the nipped waist. The long sleeves opened longitudinally at the armholes and flowed down, folding back to expose her arms whenever she moved them. The skirt was bell shaped in the front with a detachable ten-foot train at the waist that folded softly at the back with pleats of tulle.

The bodice below the décolleté, with that newly installed azure-satin inlay, was embellished in prominent silver flower wreaths, and the borders of the sleeves and train, as well as the middle of the bodice and skirt, were all embroidered in complex golden garlands. A panel of gold velvet traveled down the midfront with pearl and diamond buttons, and the *kokoshnik,* the headdress that stood for a veil, was exquisite snow-white lace worked with the same designs.

Cali let out a ragged breath, still hardly believing her own eyes. "I don't think I could have gotten into this thing if you weren't here, Kass."

"I trust Maksim will know how to get you out of it?" Kassandra chuckled, then frowned in alarm. "Do you get how we put it on you to instruct him if he runs into trouble? If he gets frustrated being unable to peel it off you and damages it, I'd…"

"Yeah, have an ulcer."

"Ulcer is for makeup smudges," Kassandra scoffed. "For an actual tear? Nothing less than an aneurysm."

Cali's heart slammed painfully against her ribs.

Of all the things to mention, why would Kassandra say this specifically? Was this more than a coincidence? The fates telling her something through her unwitting friend…?

Just how ridiculous was she being? People blurted out things like this all the time. It was she who was hypersensitive to it.

Her smile wavered as she met the other woman's eyes in the mirror. "Shall we let my sisters be the ones to help with the headdress and accessories?"

"Yeah, they can help with all the indestructible articles. And let's have Phaidra twist your hair up like her own hairdo. It'll suit you and the accessories perfectly."

Even in her lingering dismay, she smiled at Kassandra's

protectiveness of the dress, which only a true artist would feel toward an irreplaceable work of art.

The others' reaction to her appearance confirmed that she looked like a totally different woman. Her sisters, especially Melina, as her eldest sister, went all teary eyed at the sight of the baby of the family looking like an empress, and basically *becoming* an empress of the new world, since her groom was an emperor of industry and commerce.

As they gathered around her, Kassandra stopped them from hugging her so *their* makeup and perfume wouldn't stain the dress. Teasing Kassandra about her new obsession, they started adorning Cali in the jewelry Kassandra insisted *had* been that particular dress's, especially the breathtakingly ornate crown of white gold, pearls and diamonds.

Then it was time. To marry Maksim.

She rushed out of the suite as fast as the dress allowed her with the rest behind her, trying to help her with her train, then giving up because she needed no help at her speed, since it flew behind her on the marble floors of the mansion.

They had to pull her back at the entrance of the dance hall so she wouldn't spill in. She forced herself to walk in as if she weren't a mass of excitement and screaming nerves.

And she found herself stepping into a place she felt she'd never seen before. It had been transformed into a scene from the most sumptuous times of imperial Russia. The paneled-in-gold walls gleamed under the combined lights of the crystal and gold-plated metal sconces hanging between them and the spotlights that were directed toward the thirty-foot painted ceiling, reflecting on the scene to drench it in magical golden glow.

Against each side of the length of the gigantic rectangular hall, endless tables were set, leaving the rest of the elaborate hardwood floor empty, with only an aisle running down its middle. The tables were covered by an organza tablecloth with the symbol of the estate—a cross between a phoenix and an eagle with its wings spread—repeated in a pattern throughout. Tatjana had told her that the extravagant sets adorning the tables came from a service of Sevres porcelain Napoleon Bonaparte had given to Tsar Alexander. There were only about three hundred people seated there, with the rest of the guests attending the reception/birthday afterward.

Among those, she looked for one person first. Andreas.

It was actually hard to believe he'd come for her wedding, when he hadn't for Leonidas's funeral.

She didn't look long. He stood out in the bright, festive scene, emanating his own deep shadows. He wasn't sitting with the rest; he was standing almost at the entry, apart, alone. And, as always, he looked like a barely leashed predator, his black hair and eyes matching the darkness he exuded.

He met her eyes across the distance, didn't smile. Then he raised his hand and placed it flat over his heart.

Her nerves jangled. She loved Andreas but had never figured him out—or if her emotions were reciprocated, if he even felt anything for anyone. This simple gesture somehow told her everything he'd never said. He did love her—and probably loved the rest of his siblings, too, just in his own detached, unfathomable way.

Unfortunately, she couldn't stop to savor this rare moment, had to relinquish his gaze, move on.

Tatjana captured her focus next. She was at the middle of the table to the left, looking majestic in an elaborate gold-satin dress that she believed belonged to one of Russia's grand duchesses. Rosa, in something sumptuous from Tatjana's wardrobe, was standing behind her, with an enthralled Leo in a vivid blue-and-gold miniature of an adult costume, looking so absolutely adorable her heart flailed in her chest.

She kept her eyes averted from the end of the hall. She knew Maksim was there, flooding the hall with his overpowering presence, permeating her cells with his influence. She wanted to keep him for last. There would be no looking anywhere else after she laid eyes on him.

Aristedes, in his resplendent tuxedo, strode toward her, smiling into her dazed eyes as he took her arm.

As they walked down the royal-blue-satin aisle, spread on both sides with white-and-gold rose petals, he said, "Your man throws a mean party in record time. At least I hope he does, and this isn't how he intended to celebrate a one-year-old's birthday."

She wanted to explain that this was all new, but had no more breath. Only her feet remained working on autopilot. For she had finally looked down the aisle. At Maksim. It was a miracle she remained erect.

With every step closer he came into clearer focus, inducing more tremors into her limbs and heart.

He was wearing the adult-size version of Leo's costume, imperial clothes, though she failed to pinpoint its origin. His shoulders and chest looked even more imposing than usual in a midthigh coat in vivid blue, the same hue of the inlay in her dress but many shades darker. It was embroidered exquisitely with gold thread and cord in a horizontal repetitive pattern, each ending where golden buttons closed the coat down his massive chest. At his hard waist it opened down to reveal white gold-embroidered satin pants gathered into navy-and-tan leather boots.

And then she looked up at his face, and that was when she almost fell to her knees.

The mahogany hair that now rained down to his shoulders was scraped away from his leonine forehead and gathered back into a ponytail, the severe pull emphasizing his rugged bone structure, the lupine slant of his eye and the sensual hardness of his lips.

He looked way more than heart-stopping. And he looked…hungry. She felt him devouring her from afar, felt her body readying itself for his possession, didn't know how she'd survive the time until she could have him again.

Then they reached him where he stood on the draped-in-satin, five-step platform, and Aristedes unhooked his arm from what she realized had been her spastic grip.

He held out his hand to Maksim, who gripped it in a firm handshake, then drew him into one of those sparse male hugs. Cali heard their brief exchange.

"Make her happy, Volkov," Aristedes said. *Or else* was conveyed clearly.

It was lucky she hadn't applied makeup or she would have ended up a streaked mess when she heard Maksim's answer.

"I live to make her happy, Sarantos."

The two most important men in her life parted with a final look of understanding. Then Aristedes placed her hand in Maksim's and stepped down.

Everything from the moment her groom took her hand onward went by in a dreamlike blur.

Maksim tucked her to his side as if he were afraid she'd disappear as an ornately dressed minister started reciting the marriage vows first in Russian, then in English. After she'd recited them after him in a fugue, another man stepped forward, took the minister's place and recited vows in Greek.

No longer able to manifest surprise or to deal with these spikes in emotion, she only looked up at Maksim, love and gratitude flowing from her eyes. He hugged her tighter, his eyes smoldering with passion so fierce it singed her soul.

After they'd exchanged their own vows, and he'd kissed her senseless, he held her swooning mass to his side as he gestured to someone in the distance. In moments, Rosa came rushing up the platform with Leo popping with excitement in her arms. He threw himself at both of them, but it was Maksim who had the coordination to catch him.

Holding both of them to his heart, he addressed the guests.

"Every man lives searching for a purpose in life. If he is blessed, he finds it and can dedicate his life to it. I have been blessed beyond measure. I give you my purpose, my blessings, the owners of my heart and soul and everything that I am and have. My bride, the love of my life, Caliope Sarantos Volkova, and my son and heir, Leonidas Sarantos Volkov."

Everyone stood as one, cheering and raising their glasses in a toast to the family, and Cali broke down at last, burying her face into Maksim's chest, sobbing, while Leo jumped up and down in his father's embrace and screeched in elation, as if realizing that this was a momentous moment in all their lives.

The out-of-body feeling she'd been experiencing only deepened as the celebrations continued, merging the wedding with the birthday. Maksim took her to salute their guests before heading outside the hall, where she found the rest of the mansion *was* spread with tables for the attendees, with the children converging on Leo's wonderland.

She thought she laughed with her family, chattered in Russian with Tatjana's acquaintances, joked with Maksim's business associates who wanted to know how she'd melted that iceberg. She believed she joined in dancing the *khorovod,* the Russian circle folk dance, which her family eventually turned into the *pidikhtos,* Crete's version of the dance.

Then she was hugging and kissing endless bodies and faces, the only ones she'd remember later being her family, especially Andreas, who promised he'd come visit her… sometime.

Then she was held high in Maksim's arms, swept through the mansion to a wing she hadn't been in before. As she peeked over his shoulder, she found Kassandra and Selene running to keep up with his urgent strides. A beaming Kassandra explained with gestures that they were coming to get her out of the dress. Seemed she'd taken Maksim aside and convinced him to recruit her for the chore.

Inside a suite that Maksim had lavishly prepared for their wedding night, he reluctantly set her down on her feet, thanked Kassandra and Selene then whispered in her ear that he'd be waiting for her inside and strode away.

After a giggling Kassandra and Selene helped her out of the dress, Kassandra worshipped it back onto its hanger and Selene gave her a package that had been waiting on a coffee table. Then with one more hug, both ladies disappeared, leaving her standing in her lacy underwear and high-heeled sandals.

Cali's hands shook as she opened the package, which Maksim must have commissioned Kassandra to get for her. Inside was the most luxuriously erotic getup she'd ever seen.

Trembling all over with anticipation, she substituted it for her underwear, a dream of brilliant pearl-white stretch lace and satin that cupped her breasts into a deep cleavage and showcased the rest of her to the best advantage.

Unable to wait to see its effect on Maksim, she teetered inside, wishing he hadn't changed into anything himself, since she'd spent the whole evening dreaming of stripping him out of that costume. Yet part of her was also wishing that he *had* already disrobed, since she couldn't wait until she had his flesh beneath her hands and lips.

She entered a bedroom that was spread in gold and azure and lit with what must be a thousand candles. Maksim was at the far end with only those white pants on. His whole body bunched at the sight of her, like a starving predator who'd just spotted the one thing that would slake his hunger.

She almost fell to her knees when he rumbled, *"Moya zhena...nakonets."*

My wife. At last.

Maksim watched the incandescent vision that was his bride. He'd spent the previous night drowning in her. Instead of sating him, it had only roused the beast he'd been keeping on a spiked leash, fueling his addiction to searing levels.

He'd felt her equal craving all through the wedding, her impatience to continue making up for fifteen months of separation and starvation. He'd intended to drag her into the depths of passion the moment she walked in, give her what she needed, invade her, finish her, perish inside her.

Then she had glided in, and he'd called her his wife... and only when he'd said it had it fully registered.

She was his *wife*.

And what he felt now was...frightening. So much so it brought his old fears crashing down on him, paralyzing him.

But after her own moments of paralysis, when he didn't go to her, she started walking toward him, looking... celestial. It almost made him regret asking her friend to get her something made to worship her beauty. Her friend had chosen *too* well.

Then she was against him, running feverish hands and lips over his burning flesh, her eyes eating him up, her body grinding against his, pulling him down to the bed, taking him on top of her. Opening her legs for his bulk, undulating beneath him in a frenzy, she demanded him inside hers, riding her, pleasuring her, fulfilling her.

Her hands tangled in the string tying his hair back, almost tore at it as she tugged at his scalp, the exquisite pain lashing at his barely contained fervor.

Then her fingers bunched into his hair and she brought his head down to hers, his lips fusing with the fragrant, warm petals of her flesh to breathe a white-hot tremolo into his depths. *"Moy muzh."*

His every nerve fired. *My husband.*

And to have her say it in Russian. That she'd learned the language, and that well, for him…the gratitude he felt was at times…excruciating.

Spiraling, he tried to rise off her, to ration his response. But her pleading litanies to hurry, to take her, now, now, were like hammers smashing his control. Her beloved body quivered beneath his, her cherished face shuddered.

It was too much. He wanted too much. All of her. At once.

His growl sounded frightening in his ears as he sank his teeth where her neck flowed into her shoulder. She jerked and threw her head back, giving him a better bite. He took it. He was a hairbreadth from going berserk.

Then as she gazed up at him through hooded eyes, she made any attempts at curbing his passion impossible. "Show me how much you want me, Maksim." Her voice reverberated in his brain, dark and deep. Wild. "Brand me as yours, seal our lifelong pact, give me everything… take everything."

With a grunt of surrender, he freed her silky locks

from the high chignon he'd longed to demolish all evening, pulled her head to the bed for his devouring. She bombarded him with a cry of capitulation and command.

He rose to free himself from the confines of his pants, to tear that tormenting figment off her, then hissed in relief when he found her wearing nothing beneath it. His fingers slid between the lips of her core before dipping inside her, finding her flowing with readiness.

Blind with the need to ride her, he locked her thighs over his back, drove her into the mattress with a bellow of conquering lust and embedded himself inside her to her womb.

They arched back. Mouths opened on soundless screams at the potency of the moment. On pleasure too much to bear. Invasion and captivation. Completion. New, searing, overpowering. Every single time.

His roar broke through his muteness as he withdrew. She clutched at him with the tightness of her hot, fluid femininity, her delirious whimpers and her nails in his buttocks demanding his return. He met her eyes, saw everything he needed to live for. He rammed back against her clinging resistance, his home inside her. The pleasure detonated again. Her cry pierced his being. He thrust hard, then harder, until her cries stifled on tortured squeals.

Then she bucked. Ground herself against him. Convulsed around him in furious, helpless rhythms, choking out his name, her eyes streaming with the force of her pleasure.

He rode her to quivering enervation. Then showed her the extent of his need, her absolute hold over him. He bellowed her name and his surrender to her as he again found the only profound release he'd only ever had with her, convulsing in waves of pure culmination, jetting his seed into her depths until he felt he'd dissolved inside her.

Even as he sank into her quivering arms, he was harder than before. Which didn't matter. He had to let her sleep.

He tried to withdraw. She only wound herself tighter around him, clung to him.

"There will be more and more, soon and always." He breathed the fire of his erotic promise into her mouth. "Rest now. You've been awake for forty-eight hours, and I've taxed you in every possible way beyond human endurance."

She breathed her pleasure inside him, thrust her hips to take him deeper inside her. "I can only sleep if you stay inside me. I can't get enough of you, *moy dorogoy muzh*."

"Neither will I of you…ever." She was driving him deeper into bondage. And he wouldn't have it any other way.

He drove back into her and she pulsed her sheath around him until he groaned. "Tormentress. Just wait until you're rested. I'll drive you to insanity and beyond."

In response to his erotic menace, she tossed her arms over her head, arched her vision of a body, thrust her breasts against his chest and purred low with aggressive surrender. Still jerking with the electrocuting release, he turned her, brought her over him, her shudders resonating with his.

"Give me your lips, *moya zhena*."

As she gave him what he needed, her lips stilled while fused to his, exhaustion claiming her.

As she finally surrendered to slumber, totally secure and trusting in his arms, he knew.

His resurrected fears were totally unfounded. Even through the inferno of lust, tenderness and giving had permeated him. His feelings weren't forged in selfishness and dependence but fueled by the need to enrich her life, be the source of her fulfillment. His pleasure lay here, in being hers.

He took her more securely into his containment and surrendered to their union on every level. And to peace.

For the first true time in his life.

Ten

Cali stretched in the depths of utter bliss.

She wanted to never surface, to lie here on top of her Great Russian Wolf forever.

For the past four months since their wedding, she'd gone to sleep like that, after nights of escalating abandon.

But she had to wake up. She'd promised Tatjana to spend the day with her. At least she thought she had. After a night of mind-scrambling pleasure at Maksim's hands, she wasn't even sure where she was.

She actually had to open her eyes to make certain they *were* back in Russia. They'd just come back last night after a taking-care-of-business, apartment-buying stint in New York.

She'd thought this mansion had become her home, but then she'd also felt at home on their first night in their new NYC apartment. If she hadn't been certain by then, she was now. Anywhere Maksim was would always be home to her.

She propped herself up with palms flat over his chiseled chest to wallow in his splendor.

Unbelievable. That *did* just sum him up. And every moment of every day with him. She sometimes still did find herself disbelieving this was all really happening,

wondered if it was possible she'd ever get used to his…
their perfection.

But then why should she? How *could* she get used to
this? Nope. It was *im*possible. There was nothing to do,
and nothing she *wanted* to do, but live in a state of perpetual wonder.

Just looking at him had her heart trying to burst free
of its attachments and her breath refusing to come until
she drew it mingled with his beloved scent. So she did.

At the touch of her lips on his, he smiled in his sleep
and rumbled, *"Lyublyu tebya."*

She caught the precious pledge in an openmouthed kiss.

He instantly stirred, dauntingly aroused, returned the
kiss then took it over.

She gasped with pleasure as he swept her around, bore
down on her. "Love you more, Maksim."

"There's no way you love me more, *moye serdtse.* I've
waited all my life for you, knew it the moment I saw you."

She arched up, opening herself for him. "Same here."

He rose on his knees and positioned himself at her molten entrance, held her immobile by her hair for his passionate onslaught, the way she loved him to. *"Nyet,* I'm
older, so I don't only love you more, I've loved you longer."

She cried out with the searing pleasure of his words
and his plunge into her body. Their hunger was always
too urgent at first. It took only a few gulps of each other's
taste, a few unbridled thrusts to have them convulsing in
each other's arms, the pleasure complete.

After the ecstasy he drove her to demolished her completely, he twisted to lie on his back and draped her over
him again, a trembling blanket of sated flesh.

A sigh of contentment shuddered out of him after the
burst of exertion and satisfaction.

She raised an unsteady head to savor his beauty. "You're

feeling quite smug, aren't you? You think you've claimed the More and Longer Loving title for life, don't you?"

"If this ruffles your feathers too much, I can be persuaded to grant you equal billing in the 'More' category. The 'Longer' one, alas, is an unchangeable fact of time. Being the spring chick that you are, you just don't have the creds."

She drove her hands into the thick, mahogany hair that now fell past his shoulders at her demand, tugged sharply, knowing he loved it when she played rough. "Do you know what happens to condescending wolves, even the one-of-a-kind specimens?"

He stretched beneath her languidly, provocation itself. "*Da*...they get punished, with even more love and pleasure."

"Damn straight." She swooped to devour those maddeningly seductive lips, took him over this time, tormented and inflamed and owned every inch of him until she had him begging her to ride him. And she did. Hard and long, until they both almost shattered with pleasure.

Afterward, tingling with aftershocks, she let him haul her to the shower, where they spent an indeterminable time leisurely soothing and pampering each other.

They'd just exited the bathroom guffawing as he chased her to tickle her when a knock came on the door.

She bolted away from Maksim's groping hands and started jumping into her clothes. "Leo! Hurry, put something on."

He picked up his jeans, his smile unfettered. "Our son has an impeccable sense of timing. He lets us feast on each other in peace, then comes to join in for playtime."

She prodded him along and he shoved himself with difficulty into his jeans, wincing and muttering that only *un*dressing was safe with her around.

Her wide grin of triumph elicited a growled promise of retribution as she rushed to the door.

As soon as she opened it, Leo bolted inside without even looking at her. She laughed. The wily boy was preempting her, wasn't risking her telling Rosa to take him away for now. And he was after his daddy anyway, his biggest playmate and fan.

She exchanged a few words with Rosa, setting up the day, then turned to her men, delight dancing on her lips at the sight they made together.

Leo was popping up and down with arms stretched up for his daddy to pick him up. Maksim was standing above him, looking down at him.

Her smile faltered. The sense of something wrong hit first. What it was registered seconds later.

It was the way Maksim was looking down at Leo… as…as if…

As if he didn't know him.

Even worse, it was as if Maksim wasn't even aware *what* Leo was, where or who *he* was…

A bolt of ice froze her insides wholesale. Her heart exploded from the rhythm of serenity to total chaos.

"Maksim…?"

His eyes rose to her and what she saw there almost had her heart rupturing. Horror. Helplessness.

Then he collapsed…like a demolished building. As if every muscle holding him up had snapped, every bone had liquefied.

"Maksim!"

Her scream detonated in her chest and head, its sheer force almost tearing them apart. Hurling herself across the room, she barely caught him, slowing down his plummet before he keeled over Leo, desperation infusing manic strength into her limbs.

Shuddering, she crumpled with Maksim's insupportable deadweight to the ground, barely clearing Leo, who'd frozen to the spot, eyes stricken, fright eating through his incomprehension by the second. Any moment now he'd realize this was no game. Any moment now Maksim would…would…

She screamed for Rosa, a scream that must have rocked the mansion, bringing Rosa barging into the suite in heartbeats.

She heard herself talking in someone else's voice, rapid, robotic. "Get my phone, take Leo away, keep everything from Tatjana for now, get Sasha. *Go*."

She'd lived through a dress rehearsal of this catastrophe a thousand times in her mind. Leaving nothing up to chance, Maksim had coached her in the exact measures she'd take in case the worst happened. This constant dread had been the only thing polluting her psyche, eating away at her stamina. But the more time that had passed without even the least warning signs, the more she'd hoped it would never come to pass.

But it had. It *had*.

His aneurysm had ruptured.

Keeping her dry-as-rock eyes on Maksim's wide-open, vacant ones, she speed-dialed Maksim's emergency medical hotline. As per the plan, they assured her a helicopter would be there within minutes. The specialists he'd elected to handle his case would be waiting at the medical center of his choice.

Then she waited. Hit bottom, went insane over and over, waiting. Her heart had long been shredded, but it kept flapping inside her like a butchered bird only because Maksim's heart still beat powerfully beneath her quaking arms. The rest of him was inert. Feeling his vigor vanished, his very *self* extinguished, was beyond horrifying.

Those eyes where his magnificent, beautiful soul resided had emptied of everything that made him himself. Then it got worse.

At one point, something came across them, something vast and terrible spreading its gloom, eclipsing their suns. Something like anguish. No…regret. Then his lips moved in a macabre parody of their usual purpose and grace. His voice was also warped, sending more gushes of terror exploding through her.

She thought he said, *"Izvinityeh."*

Forgive me.

Then his eyes closed.

And she screamed and screamed and screamed.

She didn't stop screaming, she thought, until the medics arrived. Once there was something to do, solid steps to be taken, a switch was thrown inside her, shutting down the hysteria of powerlessness. And the rehearsed drill took her over once again.

She talked to him all the time they installed their resuscitation measures on the short flight to the state-of-the-art medical center he'd erected in the city. She told him all the good news she could—that his vitals were strong, that he had gone into shock and his whole body was flaccid, but he wasn't exhibiting any hemiparesis, which would indicate neurological damage. She told him she was there and would *never* leave his side, that he had to fight, for Leo, for his mother. But mainly for her.

She couldn't live without him.

Then they arrived at the hospital and the perfectly oiled machine of intervention he'd put in place months ago took over. She ran beside his gurney as he was taken to the O.R., but the doctors, as per his orders, wouldn't let her scrub in or watch the surgery from the gallery.

Unable to waste time arguing, she succumbed, but wouldn't be convinced to go to the waiting area. She collapsed in front of the O.R. where the man who embodied her heart and soul would be cut open, where he would struggle to stay alive. She had to be as close as possible. He would feel her, and she would be able to transfer her very life force unto him to keep him alive, to restore him.

And she wept. And realized that she'd never truly wept before. *This* was weeping, feeling her insides tearing, her psyche shattering, her very being dissolving and seeping out of her in an outpour that could never be stemmed. Only Maksim, only an end to his danger, could stop the fatal flow.

In the unending torment of waiting, she registered somewhere in her swollen, warped awareness that Aristedes and Selene had come. Their very presence reinforced the horror of what she already knew, counting the minutes since Maksim had been taken into the O.R. He'd been in there for over twelve hours.

After failing to make her get off the ground, they'd sat down there beside her, respecting her agony, trying to absorb it in the solidarity of their silence.

"Mrs. Volkov."

That voice. She'd know it among a million.

Maksim's neurosurgeon.

She shot up to her feet. But her legs had disappeared. With a cry of chagrin, she collapsed back down. Aristedes caught her, Selene shooting up to help him support her.

The moment she could feel her legs again, she pushed them away and staggered to Dr. Antonovich. This was hers alone to hear, to bear. Just like Maksim was hers alone.

Dr. Antonovich talked quickly as she approached him, as if afraid she'd attack him if he didn't. "Mr. Volkov made it without incident through surgery. He's in inten-

sive care now, where he will stay for the next two weeks
as we monitor him."

Alive. *He was alive.* He'd survived this catastrophe
that had been casting its dreadful shadow over their lives.

But… "What—what is his condition now?"

Dr. Antonovich attempted to take her arm, to support
her as she swayed. She shook her head, needing only answers, facts.

Nodding with understanding, he began quietly, "During his last checkup six months ago, the aneurysm had
still been located where attempts to approach it would
have caused serious brain damage or even death. But in
the interim, it had expanded downward, which at once
caused it to rupture, and enabled us to try a new kind of
treatment through a noninvasive, endoscopic trans-nasal
approach. I'm happy to report the aneurysm has been totally resected and the artery fully repaired."

She absorbed the information rabidly. But it still didn't
tell her what to expect next. "What about prognosis?"

"Since his aneurysm was posttraumatic, Mr. Volkov
has no underlying weakness in his vessels, and the possibility of recurrence is nil. While that is great news, it
was the rupture of the original aneurysm that we had worried about. To tell you the truth, with Mr. Volkov's general condition in the months after his accident, I had little
hope he'd survive a rupture. The last time he came in six
months ago, he'd shown little physical progress. But the
man I operated on today was the most robust person I've
ever seen. If I had to hazard a guess, I'd say you're the
reason behind his miraculous improvement."

Maksim had said that. That she and Leo were a magical elixir, that being with them—with *her*—had revital-
ized him, gave him new capacities and limitless strength.

It had been why she'd let her guard down, believing nothing would happen to him.

"What does his general condition have to do with his prognosis?" she choked out.

"Everything. Apart from the neurological condition after rupture, it's what decides the prognosis. As a surgeon who deals almost exclusively in cerebral accidents, I almost never give optimistic percentages. But with Mr. Volkov in superb physical condition, if the next two weeks pass without incident, I believe he has an over ninety percent chance of making a full recovery."

She pounced on him, digging her shaking hands into his arms. "What can I do? Tell me there's something I can do."

He extricated himself gently, took her arm. "You can keep on doing exactly what got him to this state of superb health. And once he clears the sensitive postoperative period, both of you can forget about this uncertain phase of your lives."

She stopped, the tears that hadn't slowed during their conversation flowing faster. "Wh-when can I see him?"

The surgeon ventured a faint smile. "Mr. Volkov has instructions firmly in place about every possible development of his condition. You and anyone you indicate are to have full access to him, night or day, as long as there is no medical reason not to. You can even stay with him in ICU."

She grasped his arm again. "I—I can?"

The man nodded. "He funded the whole hospital, and keeps upgrading it at our request with the latest technology. The only thing he ever asked for in return was that, if he ever needed our services, we would arrange for you to stay with him while he recuperates, if that was what you wanted…."

And she broke down, the agony of loving him and fearing for him, demolishing her. "I want… God, oh, God… I want…I want nothing else in the world…*please.*"

The first three days, Cali stayed by Maksim's side around the clock, counting his breaths, hanging on to the exact shape of his heartbeats and brainwaves. There was no change whatsoever. His vitals remained strong and steady, but he didn't regain consciousness.

The only reason she didn't go berserk was that the doctors insisted he was sleeping artificially. He'd been sedated to give his brain the chance to recover during this sensitive phase, when awareness would tax it. Dr. Antonovich was being extra careful, as she'd begged him to be, even if it freaked her out of her mind to see her indomitable Maksim so inert.

It was amazing how perfect he looked. The noninvasive technique had left his hair untouched, and it appeared as if he were sleeping peacefully, whole and healthy.

On the fourth day, they let him wake up. For one hour in the morning and another in the evening.

That first time he opened his eyes, she almost died of fright. The blank look he gave her had nightmares tearing into her mind. Of amnesia…or worse.

Then his gaze filled with recognition. Before jubilation could take hold, gut-wrenching emotion surged to the surface and the tears that constantly flowed gushed. She kissed him and kissed him, telling him she loved him, loved him, loved him, that she'd always, *always* be beside him, would never, ever leave his side, and that it was only a matter of time before they had their perfect life back.

He made no response as she talked and talked until she was terrified *he* couldn't talk. At last he told her he was just tired, then listlessly turned his head away and closed his eyes. She didn't think he slept, just kept his eyes shut. Until they'd come and put him under again.

When she'd pursued Dr. Antonovich with her report of his first weird waking episode, he said it was natural for Maksim to wake up groggy and not all there. When she insisted he'd been neither, just…blunted, he'd gone on to explain the obvious, that the brain was an unpredictable organ and she'd have to play it by ear, let him go through his recovery in his own pace and not worry, and mostly not let him feel her anxiety.

Determined to take the surgeon's advice, she told herself that anything she felt was irrelevant. Hard facts said Maksim was neurologically intact. And that was far more than enough. If it took him forever to bounce back from this almost lethal ordeal, it would be a price she'd gladly pay.

And he did bounce back, faster than his surgeon's best hopes. The two weeks in ICU became only one, with everyone, starting with Tatjana and Leo, coming to visit during his waking hours at his request. He was transferred to a regular suite and the sedation was confined to the night hours; then even that was withdrawn. By the next week, the surgeon saw no reason to keep him in hospital, discharged him with a set of instructions for home care and follow-ups, but gave him a clean bill of health.

But Maksim was subdued, only exhibiting any spark around his mother and son. With them he was almost his old self. Cali kept telling herself she was imagining things, and that even if she wasn't, there was a very good reason for this.

He was depleted, out of sorts, had just survived a near-fatal medical crisis and must be shaken to the core. But he couldn't show any of this to Tatjana and Leo. He hadn't even told his mother of his condition in fear of worrying her, and would now do anything to reassure her of his return to normal. He also wouldn't risk scarring Leo's young and impressionable psyche by allowing any of his post-traumatic stress to rise to the surface around him.

But around her? He could let his true condition show without having to bear the effort of putting on an act, and he could count on her to understand.

And she did understand. She only missed him. *Missed* him.

He was there but not there. He talked to her, especially when others where around, and she did feel his gaze on her sometimes, but the moment she turned to him, starving for connection, he looked away and sent her spiraling back into deprivation.

But she would persevere. Forever if need be. That was her pledge to him.

For better or for worse. For as long as she lived.

Three months after Maksim's discharge from the hospital, Cali's resolve was starting to waver.

Instead of things getting better, if even slightly, they only got worse.

The proof had come two weeks ago, when Dr. Antonovich had given him the green light to resume all his normal activities without reservations. It was as if he'd released him from a prison he'd been dying to break free of. He'd hopped onto a plane and gone on a business tour…alone.

He *had* called regularly during the past two weeks to reassure them, but called her own phone only when his mother didn't pick up. Even when he did, he said nothing personal, let alone intimate, just asking about Leo or asking her to put him through.

On the day he was supposed to come back, she'd run

out of rationalizations. There was no escaping the one possible conclusion anymore.

He was avoiding her.

And for the first time since she'd laid eyes on him, she dreaded seeing him, meeting his gaze. Or rather having him escape meeting hers again.

Just minutes later, he walked into the living room, where they were all gathered waiting for him. And the sight of him felt like a stab through her heart.

He'd lost weight since his crisis, understandably. But it wasn't only that his clothes hung around him that hurt. It was what felt like a statement that he'd withdrawn his emotional carte blanche to her.

He'd cut his hair.

It was now even shorter than when she'd first seen him across that reception hall—almost cropped off.

She felt catapulted back in time, only worse. Back then his eyes had smoldered with hunger; now they only filled with heaviness.

She still rushed to join in welcoming him, only to feel the white-hot skewer in her gut turning when he slipped away from her embrace, pretending to answer Leo's demand for his attention. She sat there with the talons pinning her smile up for Tatjana's and Leo's sake, sinking into her flesh and soul with every passing moment, until Leo fell asleep and Tatjana excused herself for the night. With just a curt good-night, Maksim walked out, too.

And she reached breaking point.

She had to know what was wrong or she'd lose her mind.

Forcing herself to follow him, dreading another brush-off, she approached the suite he'd moved to since he'd gotten out of hospital, with the excuse that he was suffering from bouts of insomnia at night and didn't want to disturb her.

Tiptoeing in, she found him sitting on the edge of a chair in the sitting area, his elbows resting on his knees, his cropped head held in his hands, his large palms covering his face. His shoulders, now looking diminished, were hunched over, his whole pose embodying the picture of defeat.

Her heart did its best to tear itself out of her chest.

A burst of protectiveness welled up inside her, had her running toward him, desperately needing to ward off whatever was weighing him down. His head snapped up at her approach, and for moments, she saw it. The unguarded expression of…torment.

Crying out with the pain of it, she hugged him fiercely, withdrawing only to hold his face in trembling hands, rain kisses over his face, his name a ragged litany, a prayer on her lips.

After only moments, he pulled away, his hands clamping hers, taking them away from his face. Her heart twisted in her chest at his clear and unequivocal rejection.

"I'm not ready for this."

This. Her nearness? Her emotions? What was…*this?*

She pried her hands from his warding grip, the sick electricity of misery that had become her usual state erratically zapping in her marrow. "Dr. Antonovich said you might suffer from some mood swings for a while."

He heaved up to his feet. "I'm suffering from nothing."

"This was a major trauma and surgery in your most vital organ. It's only expected you won't bounce back easily."

"He gave me a clean bill of health. There's nothing wrong with me. Just because I'm not up for sex doesn't mean I'm malfunctioning."

It felt like he'd backhanded her.

Was that how abused people felt? Would a physical blow have hurt more?

"I didn't say that," she choked. "And I'm not asking for sex or expecting it. I just want to…"

"You just want to touch me and kiss me. You want me to show you intimacy and emotion, what I showed you from the time I came back till the aneurysm ruptured." His voice hardened. "I tried to show you that I don't want any of that anymore, but you won't take a hint."

"It's all right. I understand…"

"You don't," he bit off. "You don't *want* to understand."

She swallowed back the sobs, unable to bear his harshness, which she'd never before been exposed to.

Then she remembered. "Dr. Antonovich said there was a chance for some personality changes…"

"There are no changes. This is me. The *real* me."

His growl fell on her like a wrecking ball. A lightning bolt of understanding.

"You mean it wasn't the real you before? Since your accident? Since you came back?"

He made no answer. And that was the most eloquent one.

"You mean when you left me, it was because you wanted nothing more to do with me? Then you had the accident, and thinking you'd die any moment made you vulnerable, made you need intimacy, to reaffirm your life? Or even worse, that aneurysm was pressing on your brain, causing your radical personality change. And once it was treated, you reverted to your real self, the self that didn't love me, that left me without a backward glance?"

The dismal darkness in his gaze said he hated hearing that. Because it was true. Because he felt terrible about it, but couldn't change it. He couldn't force himself to love her when he no longer felt anything.

His love for her had been injury induced. Now that he'd been fixed, he'd been cured of it.

She still had to hear him say it. "Do you want me to leave?"

His eyes were suddenly extinguished, as if everything inside him had just turned off, died. "I…think it would be best."

She'd hoped…until the words had left his mouth.

Her whole being lurched with agony so acute she caved under its onslaught; her face, her insides, all of her felt like a piece of burned paper crumbling in a careless hand.

One thing was still left unsaid. Not that it would change anything. It just had to be said.

"I'm…pregnant."

He nodded as if he, too, barely had enough life force to sustain him. "I know."

So he knew. Nobody had noticed as she'd lost so much weight. But he knew her intimately…as he no longer wanted to know her. As he seemed unable to contemplate knowing her.

"What I told you over two years ago stands."

About supporting her and his child. His *children* now.

She'd be a single parent now, not to one but two children. After she'd known what it was to share a child with him.

And she wailed, "Why did you ever come back? Why didn't you just leave me in my ignorance of what it could be like?"

He wouldn't look at her as he rasped, "I can't change the past, but this is better for the future, Caliope. I know you don't need anything, but you and…the children would still have everything that I have, and would have all my support in any way you'll allow. If you still let me be Leo's father, and the new baby's when it's born, you don't have to see me, too. In fact, I'd rather you didn't."

And the heart that had already been shattered was pulverized. "Did you *ever* love me, Maksim?"

He sat down heavily in his chair, throwing his head back, squeezing his eyes. "Don't dredge everything up, Caliope. Don't do this to yourself."

"I have to. I must make sense of this or I'll go insane."

He opened his eyes, looked at her with a world of dejection and said nothing.

No. He'd never loved her.

There was nothing more to say. To feel. To hope for.

She turned and walked away.

At the door, she felt compelled to turn back.

Strange how he still looked like the man she loved. The man who'd loved her. When that man had never existed.

"Since you told me of your aneurysm, I lived in fear of losing you. Now that I have, I'm only glad I didn't lose you to death. Even though I feel like a widow."

And she said goodbye. To the man who never was. To happiness and love and everything hopeful and beautiful she'd never have again.

Back in her suite, she stepped into the shower cubicle and stood limply beneath the powerful spray as the water changed from punishingly cold to hot, shudders spreading from her depths outward.

She squeezed her eyes, needing tears to flow, to release some of the unbearable pressure. None came. She'd depleted every last one and would forever be deprived of their relief.

Waves of despair almost crushed her, shudders racking

her so hard until she could no longer stand, and she sank in an uncoordinated heap to the cubicle's marble floor.

She lay there for maybe hours.

At last she exited the shower, dressed, packed her bags, gathered a bewildered Leo and Rosa and swept them back to New York.

Eighteen hours later, she entered her old building's elevator. She'd sent Leo with Rosa for the night.

She was…finished, didn't want to expose her son to more of her anguish. He'd felt it all through the flight, had fussed and wailed most of it. He must have also felt she was taking him away from his daddy.

Not that she would. Maksim would come for Leo, and she'd let him see him every day if he wanted. Despite everything, one thing was undeniable: Maksim loved his son. It had nothing to do with whatever he felt…or rather, *didn't* feel for her. That father/son bond hadn't been the aneurysm's doing, so it had survived its removal.

It was her love that had been so superficial, so artificial, it had vanished at the touch of a scalpel.

The ping of the elevator lurched through her. She stumbled out, walked with eyes pinned to the ground. She'd have to sell the apartment. Too many memories with Maksim here. She had to purge him from her life. If she hoped to survive.

Then she raised her eyes…and he was there.

He'd been sitting on the ground by her door, was now rising to his feet. Her legs gnarled together. And he was there, stopping her from plummeting to the ground.

Her eyes devoured him for helpless moments before common sense kicked in. "Leo… He's not with me…."

"I know. I'm here to talk to you."

And she panicked, pushed frantically out of his supporting arms. "No. No, no, *no.* You can't keep reeling me in, shredding me apart, throwing me out then doing it again. I won't let you do this to me. Not again. Not ever again."

Caliope's words fell on Maksim like fists dipped in ground glass…smashing into his heart and brain.

But he had to do this. He had to make her understand.

Taking the keys from her limp hands, he opened her door, urged her inside. "I have to talk to you, Caliope. After this, you'll never have to see me again."

The defeat and despair in her eyes made him wish again that he'd died on that operating table.

"It's you who doesn't want to see me, Maksim. You've reverted to your true nature, but I'm the same person who's always loved you, who can't stop loving you. I wish there was some medical procedure that would keep me from feeling like this, but if there were, I couldn't have it, because of Leo and the baby. You said you'd rather not see me again, and you were right. I *can't* see you again. Just thinking of you makes my sanity bleed out. Just looking at you makes my blood congeal inside my arteries with grief. If you want your children to have a mother and not a wreck, you won't let me see you again."

He deserved all that and more. But he had to do this.

He caught her arm as she turned away. "I left you once without explanations. I have to explain this time."

"I don't want your explanations. I don't care *why* you're killing me. It won't change the fact that you're killing me all the same."

He groaned, "Caliope…"

She stepped away unsteadily. "Okay, that was over the top. I am too strong to shrivel up and die. I will regain my equilibrium and go on. For myself as well as for my children."

His hands fisted, cramping with the need to reach for her. "This is what I want you to do. To move on, to forget…"

"You don't get to tell me what you want anymore," she cried out, strangled, shrill. "You don't get to pretend you care about what happens to me. I don't want to move on, and I don't want to forget. It if weighs on your conscience, I can't help you there. The man I love exists here—" she thumped her chest hard with her fist, face shuddering, eyes welling "—and here." Another jarring punch against her temple, her whole frame quaking with the rising tide of misery. "*He's* in my senses and reflexes, *he's* part of my every cell. Even if you're not him anymore, you can't take *him* away from me, so the new you can feel better…"

His own torment burst out of him on a butchered groan. "I was aware all the time after I collapsed, Caliope."

That brought her tirade to an abrupt end.

He went on. "All through the trip to the hospital, up to when they forced you, per my orders, to stay out of the O.R. I saw, *felt everything.* I was *mutilated* by what it did to you when I collapsed. I've never seen anyone so…wrecked, known someone could suffer so totally, so horrifically. And I realized that I'd done that to you. I've been far more selfish than you once accused me of being, involving you in this doomed relationship, where I get to have the happiness and blessing of your love as long as I live, only to leave you with the anguish of my loss and the curse of my memory."

Tears still cascading down her cheeks, she gaped at him.

"Dr. Antonovich might say he's over ninety percent certain I'm fully recovered, but there is still a percentage I'm not. And I can't bear making you live in constant dread waiting for me to collapse again, and maybe this time not making it…or worse."

Her tears suddenly stopped. Everything about her seemed to hit pause.

Then a cracked whisper bled out of her. "You mean you did love me? And never stopped?"

There was no way he could stop the admission now. "I've loved you from the first moment I saw you. I don't think I can stop loving you, even if they remove my whole brain."

This time her voice was more audible as her eyes became fiercely probing. "And you decided it was better for me to lose you while you were still alive? That's why you pulled away after your surgery, to build up my resentment toward you, so that if you eventually died it wouldn't hurt me as much?" His nod was wary, the dreadful feeling he'd botched this whole thing creeping up his spine. "Then why did you follow me here? Wasn't my leaving what you were after?"

His breath left him in a strangled rasp. "I've been trying to make you opt for saving yourself. I wanted you to walk out angry and indignant, intending to put me behind you. But you were *demolished* instead, without any hope of getting over me. *Bozhe moy*…the last things you said, about going insane not knowing…about feeling like a widow. What you said now…about loving me no matter what…"

He felt totally lost, no longer knowing what he was here to do or how he could possibly get her to save herself.

He tried again. "I couldn't leave you without an explanation again. I couldn't bear letting you keep on thinking I didn't love you. I love you so much, love our family and our lives together, I can't breathe with it most of the time. But I *can't* expose you to heartbreak of this magnitude again."

A long, full moment dragged by, then her murmur sounded more like the Caliope he knew. "One final question. If I were the one who got injured or crippled, would you abandon me?"

"Caliope, *nyet*..."

She plowed on. "If you knew I would possibly die at any moment, would you give up one single day with me now, live whatever time I had left apart from me to save yourself the anguish you'd feel if I died while we were in utmost closeness?"

Feeling his brain simmering, his eyes filling with acid, he protested, his voice a ragged, broken moan. "I'd give my very life for any time at all with you. For a month. A day. An *hour.* And nothing would ever take me away from your side if you love me, no matter what."

"Something *is* taking you away, when I love and need you, right now. You. You're the one who keeps depriving me of you."

And he realized. He hadn't only spoiled his mission, he'd closed the trap shut behind him...and her.

"*Bozhe moy,* Caliope, dying or worse, living crippled, is far preferable to me to hurting you. But whatever I do, I'll end up hurting you, and I thought..." He exhaled roughly. "I no longer know what I thought. Everything worked out in my mind when I was trying to drive you away...then I saw and felt the reality of your pain, and knew it wouldn't just end if I made you leave..."

He stopped, stared at her helplessly, loving her so much it overpowered him, defeated him.

And she gently drew him to her, clasping him into heaven, her supple arms sheltering him, taking him away from all his fears and uncertainty. "Then just accept your fate, Maksim, being mine for the rest of our lives, however long that will be. Just be ecstatically happy and humbly thankful, like I am, for every second we have together. Stop trying to save me future pain and only hurting me now and forever. Start loving me again and let me breathe again."

And just like that, every last shackle of anxiety snapped and every insurmountable barrier of dread came crashing down.

He surged around her, crushed her in his arms. "I can never stop loving you. I *won't* stop loving you even when I stop breathing. You are my breath, in my every cell, too. My heart beats to your name, my senses clamor for your being. I am yours, and I beg you to never let me go."

Her tears flowed again, this time of joy, of healing, drenching his chest, cleansing his soul. "I've never once let you go, mister. I've been clinging to you with all I have, but you're the one who keeps leaving every time your misguided chivalry and skewed self-sacrificing tendencies act up."

"If I ever stray again, out of any new bout of stupidity, club me over the head and drag me back into your embrace."

Her lips trembled in a smile of such acute love, he dropped his head in her bosom and let his tears flow.

Her hands shook over his head, sifting through his now bristly, short hair. "Mmm... I can and will carry out the clubbing part, but you're no longer a good candidate for being dragged back where you belong. No hair."

His laugh choked in his crowded chest. "That hair is growing back, waist length if you like."

"Ooh, I like." She leaned back in the circle of his arms. "And I want, Maksim, and need...and crave. Three months without you has taken me through all the stages of starvation."

"Can I dedicate the next thirty years to rectifying my major crime of three months of tormenting you in vain?"

She clung around his neck. "Make it fifty and you're on."

Feeling he'd just closely escaped an eternal plummet into hell, he swept her to bed, where he reunited them flesh in flesh, never to be sundered again.

And this time he knew that any lingering anxiety would only serve to intensify their union, make them revel in and appreciate each second they had together even more. If this wasn't survivable, who cared? Life itself ended, but this, their love, never would.

When the storm of passion had abated after a long night of wild abandon, he rose over her, caressing her from buttock to back, marveling in her beauty, wallowing in her hold over him. "Can we go retrieve our little lion cub now?"

She arched sensuously, the very sight of contentment. "Oh, yes. He's desolate without his dada. And Maksim…"

"Da, moy dusha?"

"If our baby is a boy, I want to name him Mikhail. If it's a girl, Tatjana Anastasia."

He buried his face in her neck, groaning, "You'll really kill me with too much love."

"I want to make you live like you never did."

And he told her what he'd once thought and never put it into words to her. "You do. Without you, I existed. With you, I'm alive, alight. I don't think I'll ever find enough ways to thank you for that, to show you how much I love you."

"When you weren't showing me you love me by leaving me, you did wonders."

Feeling beyond humbled by her blessing, he cupped her precious cheek. "For showing me the good inside of me, for giving me the best of everything, for loving me even when I made it impossible, for never giving up on me until I got it right...I promise you, you've see nothing yet."

His own personal pieces of heaven shone with tears and adoration. "I'll hold you to that. And I'll hold on to you. I'm never letting you go again."

"Never again, *moya zhena, moya dusha*," he pledged. "Never, my wife, my soul. This time, forever."

* * * * *

Don't miss USA TODAY *bestselling author Olivia Gates's next book,* SEDUCING HIS PRINCESS, *a* MARRIED BY ROYAL DECREE *novel, coming March 2014 from Harlequin Desire.*

If you liked this BILLIONAIRES & BABIES *story, don't miss the next book in this #1 bestselling Harlequin Desire series,* A BILLIONAIRE FOR CHRISTMAS, *by* USA TODAY *bestselling author Janice Maynard!*

REQUEST YOUR FREE BOOKS!

2 FREE NOVELS PLUS 2 FREE GIFTS!

◆ HARLEQUIN®

Desire

ALWAYS POWERFUL, PASSIONATE AND PROVOCATIVE

YES! Please send me 2 FREE Harlequin Desire® novels and my 2 FREE gifts (gifts are worth about $10). After receiving them, if I don't wish to receive any more books, I can return the shipping statement marked "cancel." If I don't cancel, I will receive 6 brand-new novels every month and be billed just $4.55 per book in the U.S. or $4.99 per book in Canada. That's a savings of at least 13% off the cover price! It's quite a bargain! Shipping and handling is just 50¢ per book in the U.S. and 75¢ per book in Canada.* I understand that accepting the 2 free books and gifts places me under no obligation to buy anything. I can always return a shipment and cancel at any time. Even if I never buy another book, the two free books and gifts are mine to keep forever.

225/326 HDN F4ZC

Name	(PLEASE PRINT)	
Address		Apt. #
City	State/Prov.	Zip/Postal Code

Signature (if under 18, a parent or guardian must sign)

Mail to the **Harlequin® Reader Service:**

IN U.S.A.: P.O. Box 1867, Buffalo, NY 14240-1867
IN CANADA: P.O. Box 609, Fort Erie, Ontario L2A 5X3

Want to try two free books from another line?
Call 1-800-873-8635 or visit www.ReaderService.com.

* Terms and prices subject to change without notice. Prices do not include applicable taxes. Sales tax applicable in N.Y. Canadian residents will be charged applicable taxes. Offer not valid in Quebec. This offer is limited to one order per household. Not valid for current subscribers to Harlequin Desire books. All orders subject to credit approval. Credit or debit balances in a customer's account(s) may be offset by any other outstanding balance owed by or to the customer. Please allow 4 to 6 weeks for delivery. Offer available while quantities last.

Your Privacy—The Harlequin® Reader Service is committed to protecting your privacy. Our Privacy Policy is available online at www.ReaderService.com or upon request from the Harlequin Reader Service.

We make a portion of our mailing list available to reputable third parties that offer products we believe may interest you. If you prefer that we not exchange your name with third parties, or if you wish to clarify or modify your communication preferences, please visit us at www.ReaderService.com/consumerchoice or write to us at Harlequin Reader Service Preference Service, P.O. Box 9062, Buffalo, NY 14269. Include your complete name and address.

HD13R